Saved By Grace

Saved By Grace

A novel by

Cory Clubb

BAAL HAMON PUBLISHERS,
Akure, Nigeria.

www.baalhamon.com/publishers/

publishers@baalhamon.com

ISBN-10:   978-075-690-6
ISBN 13:   978-978-075-690-1
EAN: 9789780756901

Design Credits:
Front Cover Photo: Getty Images.com
Back Cover Photo: Getty Images.com
Author Photo: Hollie Clubb
Cover Design: Cory Clubb

1

A crack of thunder awoke James Mason.

In the stiff darkness, he lifted his head and tried to make out the time on his alarm clock. The blurs of red shifted together almost to make out numbers but were then taken away. Yet, just as they had quickly disappeared they instantly reappeared, and then were gone again.

Off and on, the red mixtures blinked. Finally fighting through his struggling sight, James squinted and adjusted, just enough to make out the time: 12:00 am. James blew out a breath of frustrated air as rain pitter-pattered on his windows.

At least it's only midnight.

James rolled over facing the opposite direction from his clock and stared blankly into the flashing clouds outside his window. James could hear the rustle on the street below his condo complex. The honking of impatient travelers, loud mufflers, and city buses filled his ears.

This can't be right? He thought to himself.

As another, smaller, more distant bellow of thunder rumbled, James shot open his eyes. Quickly flipping to his previous side of the bed, he settled his sight on the clock once again. The red numerals bounced in and out of color still at 12:00 am.

Oh...No.

James thrust his bed cover off his body and rushed across the polished wood floor to his dresser. Picking up his watch, he examined the hands. They read a quarter after nine. James gently closed his eyes and hung his head in disbelief. He was an hour and fifteen minutes late for work.

Racing through his now brightly lit condo, James cursed at his tardiness. He donned a light blue shirt and grey pants. With quick look in the mirror, he used his fingers to comb his blonde hair to the side. His broad shoulders drew down his lengthy body. He was not a very big man and yet he wasn't very fit either. His blue eyes, that matched his shirt and tie, darted around the room as he located his shoes. Quickly gathered his wallet and keys, he grabbed his jacket and head out for the door. James fumbled to lock his condo door, but stopped a quick second then re-entered his condo. Running toward his computer, he snatched up his cell phone in its charger and then bolted out of his home once again.

He took the stairwell, not because it was faster, but because elevators were not his favorite modes of transportation. He had a history with enclosed areas and didn't like them. Furthermore, he disliked crowd of people, cramping his personal space and sending his nerves into frenzy. But that was the least of his worries at the moment. Fumbling down the stairs and out through the side exit of the building, James trotted amongst the light rain toward his private garage space. He punched in the five-digit key code and unlocked the large door revealing his most prized possession; a 1967 Shelby GT Mustang with a 427 sideoiler engine, four speed toploader transmission, Hallibrand magnesium wheels, chrome plating that shined even at night, and fire engine red in color with double black lines down the center.

The mustang had been his father's own. It was purchased when his father's job had taken a bounce of success. His father loved the car and it was the envy of his co-workers at the work. He would spend weeknights after work, replacing parts and finishing the interior with leather. In the summer 1984, it won first prize at the county fair auto show. James remembers the times that his father and mother took him on long drives through the countryside. His father's brownish blonde hair would blow in the wind as they sped down the road. His father was a careful and thoughtful man, always wanting more out of life. He took much delight during the rides on midsummer nights. On Saturdays, James would tag along while his father washed and polished the car, mostly because he could get an ice cream cone if he was good. James loved these times because his father had to travel so much on business. James' parents were a loving couple and were very devoted to each other. His mother had long, straight dark brown hair with the eyes to match. Freckles covered her cheeks and shoulders. She was a strong-willed woman and a hard-working one. She handled the housework, bills, and taking care of James all by herself. She loved her husband and often wanted to see more of him. His father provided very well for his family with his job; yet, the tiring business trips set them apart from each other. On a Friday night in month of June in 1993, James's father was gearing up for business trip to the west coast for two weeks. Instead of leaving his wife at home this time, he asked her to go with him. The woman was so happy that tears almost came to her eyes. She questioned what they would do with James while they were away. They both talked to James about staying with his Uncle. After the discussion, they made arrangements for James to stay with his father's brother, Thomas, in his downtown apartment while the two were gone.

They left on an early morning flight and had a seven-hour trip ahead of them. James' mother squeezed him in a hug and kissed his cheek.

"You'd be good to know and listen to your uncle. Ok?" As her small mouth grew into smile and her eyes began to tear up.

"Don't worry son." said his father. "We'll, be back before you know it, and you and your uncle here will have a great time." "Make sure you look after the mustang for me; alright my boy?"

With that, he shook James's hand and gave him a wink. His father told Thomas they would call as soon as they landed. They said their goodbyes and James' parents boarded the plane.

After seeing the plane depart into the sky, James and his uncle left the airport and went about their day. James was off to school and his uncle to work. It was a little after twelve o'clock and the phone rang in Thomas's office downtown. It was the Nevada state police with troubling news.

James was in history class taking a test, when his teacher asked him to visit the main office. His uncle was waiting for him in the office. James entered the office and looked confused at why his uncle was there. Thomas' eyes looked tired and red as if he had been rubbing them.
Thomas bent down on one knee and looked James square in the face.

"Uncle Thomas what are yo u doing here?" Asked James.

"I have something very important to tell, James."
Thomas swallowed hard and blinked his eyes.
"Your parents, James...their plane...didn't make it to California."
"Oh, so they had to change planes somewhere?"
"No, James..." Thomas cleared his throat.
"Their plane crashed in Nevada." Thomas said calmly.
James gave him an innocent glance of frustration. A look of fear came over him and his face turned pale white. He stared his uncle in the eyes as tears started to well up. He tried to be

strong and hold them back, but they dripped down his face anyway.

More thunder rumbled overhead and James wiped away the rain of tears from his face. A bit of relief came over him at the sight of his automobile. James always had the notion that one day he would open the garage door and the car would not be there. Luckily today it was. Unlocking the door, James slid into the black leather interior, buckled his seat belt and started the engine. The engine turned over and hummed in perfection. A small smirk broke on James' face as he shifted into gear. Closing the garage door behind him, he sped out of the parking lot onto the street in the rain.

James' place of employment was about a good ten minutes away from his condo. He had only been working there for three months and already had a shortcut to his destination. Quickly glancing at his watch as he weaved in and out of cars above the speed limit, James groaned at the time. He would be in trouble for sure this time. He turned into a long small side street that connected with the highway. Hitting the accelerator and shifting to another gear, James flew down the road. Merging onto the deserted highway, he picked up the pace of his car and threw it into the next gear. Now more than ten miles over the set speed limit, he noticed a car ahead with its caution lights blinking.

You've got to be kidding me.

The mustang reduced its speed as it came closer and through the rain, James could see that there was a second car involved, which had slid into the ditch. James observed one woman huddling her child under an umbrella and another man was surveying the engine under her car's hood. There didn't seem to be any injuries to any of them.

What morons. James thought. *Can't they learn how to drive in the rain?*

The man glanced up and saw James's car coming. Stepping towards the other lane of the road, he started waving his arms. James sighed in disgust and barely cracked his window for the man to speak.

The man wore a tan, long trench coat over a black shirt and pants. Thick, dark glasses sat on his nose that enlarged his eyes giving him an obscure appearance. A bristly small mustache covered his upper lip in gray hairs and moved up and down as he spoke.

"I am sorry to bother you, we have just had an accident can you help us?" Pleaded the man.

James felt the weight of his cell phone in his inside pocket of his jacket. Pondered a minute and glancing at the clock on his dash replied.

"Sorry, I can't help you out. I am really in a rush."
"It won't take more than a couple of minutes." Informed the man. "Her car will not start and mine has slid into that ditch. All we need is a jump from your car to start hers again."
James took a good look at the woman's car.

A Chevy...no way am I going to let them touch my car.
"I am sorry, but I am running late for work and don't have time for this." James snarled.

At that moment, the rain started to fall harder as lightning flashed and thunder boomed. The man outside James' car now drenched in the rain removed his wet glasses and gave them a quick wipe on a dry part of his black shirt.

"I understand." Said the man, returning his glasses to his face.

He then stepped back from the car and brushed the water from his soaked forehead as he stared blankly at the classic car. James removed his foot from the brake and sped off spraying water from his tires.

The time now was 9:54 and if he hurried, he could make it to work by ten o'clock. He crushed the accelerator with his foot and the engine roared in response. Shifting the car's gears like a pro, he hit the eighty miles an hour mark on his speedometer. The car raced down the highway splashing rainwater every way. The heavy rain was hitting the windshield so much that it was blurring James' vision of the road ahead. The window wipers failed in any attempt to give him a better view. The red mustang zipped past an old early morning breakfast cafe. The restaurant had been known very well for its famous hotcakes. Yet, the small breakfast and lunch buffet style eatery unsuccessfully drew customers and didn't have many sales.

Most of all the regulars who had frequented the place were cops who usually just stopped for coffee. James thought a bit about the old cafe and its usual customers. It was too late. He could see the huge dark smudge from his rear view window slide in behind him.

They called them the Pancake Police, in respects of their eating habitat. James reduced his speed in hopes to ward off any suspicion of his hasty velocity. The blue and red lights of the squad car flashed on and James swore aloud. Grasping the stick shift, James down shifted as he slowed to frustrating stop. The cop pulled directly in after James and shined a spotlight at his vehicle. The cop sat in his cruiser for a good five minutes that felt like eternity for James. James stared vacantly again at the clock on his dashboard as it turned to ten o'clock. A knock on his window startled him and this time he rolled the window down to maximum exposure. Rain and cool wind blew on his face as he tried to focus on the police officer. In hesitation, James sputtered out.

"Listen, officer, you have to believe me sir; I know I might have been speeding a little, but I am so late for work. I need to get there as soon as possible. I haven't had this job very long and I really can't afford to lose it right now."

James waited for a response from the man.

"Sixty-five, right?" questioned the cop.

"I know, I know the limit, but like I said I woke up late and…"

The cop interjected. "No, I mean the year of the car. It's a nineteen sixty five mustang right?"

"Oh…no it's sixty seven." James explained.

"Hmm got ya. What's it do?"

"Well, 'bout one sixty an hour."

"Yep, my brother had one just like. The dang thing ran smoother then hell."

That is where James felt like he was, hell.

Rain persisted to soak the interior leather of the mustang. James rested his arm on the wet windowsill, laid his hand across his forehead and shot out a breath of air.

The officer gave a good glance around James' car and asked James for his driver's license and registration.

He then headed back toward his still flashing police car. James looked at the mess that the rain had left on the inside of the door panel.

I don't believe this.

The officer returned to the mustang and gave James back his license and registration.

"Now, you know cars like this are fun to drive fast but you are going to have to slow down." "With this rain I would hate for you to get in any kind of accident."

"Yeah." James grumbled out.

"Just be careful." The officer reminded.

The man returned to his vehicle and James turned back onto the road.

The large downtown office, where James worked, was a gigantic structure of concrete and metal. Glass windows covered almost the entire outside of it and reflected all of the surrounding buildings. "Kruger and Sons", a huge sign read on a front slab of concrete just outside of the front doors. "Corporate solutions for a corporate world" was posted right beneath the title of the company. James had always laughed at the name and trademark. Kruger didn't even have any sons, but he had three daughters. The bit of irony didn't help his mood any.

The time was 10:30 when James stepped into the lobby of the office building. Wiping the rain from his coat, he stood facing the enormous entrance.

The polished concrete tile floor rose up with marble walls to a sprawling ceiling above. Small plants as green as dollar bills stood in bare corners of the room. In the middle of the huge room sat an oak desk flanked by two revolving doors, where a receptionist was seated.

The receptionist at the desk had a scowl on her face. The forty-year-old woman was relaxed in her chair and despite others, in the lobby waiting area; she was eyeing James ever since he entered the complex. Her dyed black hair was pulled tight into a bun in the back of her head, and dark eyeliner was applied thicker than paste under her eyes. To enter the offices in the building, you had to show her your identification card. There was no way around her.

Oh great here we go. James thought.

James' cell phone rang and he answered it. It was his assistant, Peggy Davis. She squawked on and on about how he was late and had missed a meeting. James rolled his eyes in aggravation. He stepped up to the desk and fumbled his pockets for his ID badge.

"I know Peggy, Yes I know." He clarified to her.

Holding his cell phone to his ear with his left hand as he search with his right. The woman at the desk gave him a blank stare as to say, "you're wasting my time." Sickened at the gaze he was being given, James shot her one back.

"Well, do you have it?" She barked out.

"Yeah, yeah just hold on."

Peggy still rambled into James ear with annoyance as the receptionist crackled her throat. After finding his card in his inner coat pocket, he blurted out to the woman at the desk.

"Here, look here you go, are you happy?"

He presented the card right in front of her.

She kept the grimace on her face.

"Look, Peggy I will talk to you when I get up stairs."

James hung up on her, made his way through the revolving doors and up a small flight of stairs towards the stairwell.

James took his steps in anger retained from the prior incident. He huffed a few short breaths of air as the elevator dinged in arrival beside him. A couple of people exited the small unit in conversation.

"Hey, we can make room in here for you." A man quickly said holding the elevator doors ajar.

James eyed the door to the stairs and then darted his eyes toward the man.

"Oh, um, thanks, but I don't need the elevator."

"You're the new guy, James Mason, right? Fifth floor? That's a long hike up the stairs. Come on."

James started to react to the offer, but the man grabbed his arm and led him into the middle of the cramped lift. The doors closed and James could see his gold reflection in them. His face was red and he broke a sweat on his forehead.

He couldn't move. The elevator was packed. The walls started closing in on him. His palms became wet with anxiety and his breathing started to speed up. The numbers of the passing floors lit up as slowly as possible. Every ding of the skipped floors rang in his eardrums with a thud driving his brain in a panic. The elevator stopped on the third floor and opened its doors. James had to get out he couldn't take it. The same man that gave James the previous offer bumped him aside to make room for the on coming passengers.

The doors closed once again and trapped the riders in their cylinder. He could feel a brief case jabbing him in the side as the elevator shook and rattled to start up again. Now, James could feel his heart rate beat faster and faster. The small conversation in the elevator became a blocked murmur in James' ear. Everything fused to white and his vision became blurred. Sweat trickled off his body like the rain outside. James closed his eyes tight and was ready to give into the blackout that was ready to come over him. He thought to himself.

Please God help.

Just then, the doors opened on the fifth floor and James was shuffled out. A pat on his back forced his focus back to normal as sweat dripped down the side of his face.

"Hey, aren't you glad you didn't take those stairs?" Said the man from before.

James gave a small smirk as he sucked in air through his lungs. He shook his head and wiped sweat off himself. Glancing around him quickly he made way to his desk. Inside his cubicle, James sat in his chair and laid his head on his arms. He began breathing in and out at a slower pace to calm himself. His phone rang out, startling him. James looked at the caller ID on the phone it read 'Peggy Davis'. He picked up the receiver and grumbled a hello.

"Oh as I was saying before..." She squeaked. "I have those files you wanted on the Carson site and you're going to have to reschedule the meeting for this morning that you missed. The client wasn't very happy you didn't show up for it. Oh, and also Mark from press department wanted to know when the Thill Brothers website will go live."

"Peggy, please let me just have a few minutes to get my things together, alright?"

"Also, James..." She started.

"Wait Peggy wait, before you start I just asked you to give a couple of minutes did you not hear me?"

"But..." She started again.

"No, Peggy stop, don't talk. Are you deaf? Just hang up the phone."

She hung up with a small click and James did likewise. He laid his head back down on his desk. James's phone rang a second time. Picking up the receiver without looking, James snapped out his words.

"Peggy, please stop bothering me for two seconds..."

He cut short his sentence when he heard a man's voice on the other end.

"James? Are you just getting into work?" questioned the man.

James lifted his head from his desk and stared at the caller ID, it read 'Bart Hampton'.

"Yeah, yeah, I had an extremely long morning." he replied.

"Uh... have you seen Kruger, yet?"

"No, why?"

"I guess you missed a pretty important meeting this morning and he has been looking for you ever since."

"Oh, great. Just what I wanted to hear."

"Just thought I would give you a heads up."

"Yeah, thanks."

They both hung up their phones. James took a discouraged breath in and let it out. He poked his head out above his cubicle and spotted his boss' office. Closing his eyes and sitting limply back in his chair; he drew out his desk drawer and grabbed a file folder marked: Layouts. He tucked the folder under his arm, stood, and striated his tie.

The name J. R. Kruger was on a gold plate across the front of the oak door to the office. James glanced at it and shuttered. He lightly knocked on the open door and partially leaned into the office. James met eyes with his boss as he looked in. Kruger motioned for James to come in as he continued his phone conversation. His boss was an older man, but still had much of his hair on his head. His eyebrows were dark and thick and he had deep sagging bags under his eyes. He was talking on the phone in a grumbling voice. Hunched over his desk with a pen in his hand, he scribbled down notes and barking orders. A bit of spit flew from his mouth as he spoke into the phone increasing volume of his voice. James had a feeling of uneasiness come over him as he stood in front of his boss.

"I want it by the end of the day or else it will be your hide!" Shouted the man as he slammed down the phone.

Kruger rubbed his fingers on his forehead and jotted down a few more notes. He then set down his pen and folded his fingers together as he raised his eyes to James. The man squinted at James as if he was having trouble recognizing him. Kruger cleared his throat with a bit of trouble.

"Mason, how long have you been working here?"

"Almost two years…"

"And I assume that you like your job?"

James was shocked at the inquiry. Kruger stood from his chair and turned his back to him as James answered the question.
"Yes, I do."
Kruger started to pace around the office. The uncomfortable silence was nerve racking for James. He watched as his boss drew closer to him.
Finally, Kruger opened his mouth to ask another question.
"Did you know that there was a meeting today with Condit Inc?"
"Yes I did, but I can explain Mr. Kruger."
"Ok explain me this then Mr. Mason. Why did you miss the meeting that we have been preparing for the last three months?"

Now pacing even closer to James, the musky smell of the old man's after-shave wafted into his nose.
"You are supposed to be our assistant director of design. I gave you this client because I trusted you to do a good job."
Kruger spit his words at James in anger.
"You made fool out of me this morning. A fool! I am not going to have that same mistake made twice and I certainly can't have fools themselves working for me!"
James stood with his mouth open in disbelief of what was happening. He tried to speak up for himself, but couldn't find the words. Kruger still stomped around his office in madness. He stopped short right in front of James and pointed his finger at his chest.

"You're through here. I want your desk cleaned out by noon and you gone."
Kruger's phone rang and he quickly turned and returned to his desk. James stood still at the same spot in the office. He was

unmovable at the words he had just heard. Kruger glanced up at his recent ex-employee.

"Out!" He barked.

James focused back on reality and exited the office. Phones rang and laughing could be heard in the distance as James made his way to his desk. He passed a trashcan, opened it and threw the folder he had been holding into. He sat in his chair, blankly looking at his computer screen. It had taken him forever to get a job in his field of degree. All he wanted was to get a good job and start a career.

How could have this had happened? Why was this happening? He thought.

Suddenly his phone rang, it was Peggy Davis again, and James had half a thought to chew the woman out for some reason. The phone rang a second time. Gently, James took the connection cord and yanked it from the back of the phone. The power to the phone was dead in the middle of the third ring. He slumped back into his chair and buried his face in his hands.

Lightning and thunder crashed as rain poured down on James. He carried a half-full box of his belongings to his mustang. Starting the engine, he sat, wondering where his life was headed. What was he going to do? He had worked so hard to get this job in his field and now it was gone. There was no way he could get another job in the area. Not a lot of companies were hiring and how could he be so sure they would hire him. He thought for a minute about possibly going to Kruger and begging for his job back. That probably wasn't a very good idea. He slowly put the car into gear and lurched back to his condo.

James unlocked the door to his condo and entered. He found his answering machine was blinking with a missed call. He hit the play button as he threw his soaked jacket onto a chair and headed toward the bedroom. The message started to play.

"Hey, James this is Thomas I'm just checking in on you maybe we could grab lunch sometime or something, give me a call. Later"
James fell onto his bed face first. He flicked his eyes at his alarm clock. It still flashed 12:00 am. Closing his eyes, he fell asleep to the downpour of rain outside.

2

The rain outside continued to come down as Grace tucked back her blonde hair. She sat in her white walled room, on her twin bed facing a mirror. The room was very small; yet clean with certain sense of warmth. Her bed, she had had since the age of seven, sat in the middle of the room. It was made neatly and on the nightstand next to it laid an old bible and red binder notebook. The bible was bookmarked in several spots by small pieces of paper and the red binder was full of pages with her work related materials inside. Staring into her mirror a sweet smile came across Grace's face as she looked at her reflection. Her blue eyes dazzled back at her as she picked up a silver cross necklace; the One she has wore everyday; it had been her mother's own. She thought back to the day when her mother, Marie, had given it to her. Diagnosed with a fast moving breast cancer, Marie had had only one child, Grace. A few months went by and the cancer had progressed quickly than planned. Marie had been such a strong fighter yet, was becoming weak. She decided she wanted to pass away at home surrounded by her loved ones. But, before she and her family could spend any time together, she slipped into a coma. Giving up her most vital passion, communication with her daughter. Though she understood her mother was fading, Grace still sat with her. Grace could still recognize her mother through her crystal blue eyes and because she knew she was still listening, Grace would read the bible to her mother every night. Marie had very strong faith in the Lord and instilled that in her daughter.

"Always make sure Jesus is in your heart and He will lead the way."

Her mother would constantly remind her.

Marie had been in the coma for eight days now and not much was happening. But, Grace knew her mother would soon leave her.

It was a cold winter night and the Connelly house was almost completely dark, except for one room. Grace had been reading to her mother as she usually did. The light from the lamp lit up her golden locks of hair. The light blonde hair was up in two pigtails and she wore a pink nightgown that flowed to her ankles. Grace read out loud the words of the scripture.

"Love is patient, love is kind and is not jealous; love does not brag and is not arrogant, does not act unbecomingly; it does not seek its own, is not provoked, does not take into account a wrong suffered, does not rejoice in unrighteousness, but rejoices with the truth; bears all things, believes all things, hopes all things, endures all things."

A scruffy unshaven man stood at the frame of doorway to the room. His bulky appearance was covered in a stained shirt and tie. He wore baggy wrinkled pants and tan work boots on his feet. This was Frank Connelly father to Grace and husband to Marie. He listened intently, lowered his gaze to the floor in thought. Grace spotted her father in the doorway and smiled warmly at him. He motioned at the clock and gave her a wink. Grace said a prayer, kissed her mother's forehead and went to her own bedroom. Frank tucked his daughter into her bed and bent down kissing Grace's forehead. He quietly left the room and returned to his wife.

He knelt down beside her bed, staring at her motionless. He wished he could talk to her, just one more time to feel her soft words and beautiful voice. He gripped her left hand in his own and rubbed his fingers over her skin. He then rose to his dresser opened a drawer and removed a white box. Kneeling back down beside his wife, Frank opened the white box. With shaking hands, he held a small gold ring in his fingers. It shined in the light as he looked at it. Slowly and gently, he slid the ring onto his wife's finger. Again holding her hand, he dropped his head and began to weep. He listened closely to her breathing. The breaths were slow and wheezy drawn in and out from her body. Tears streamed down the man's cheeks in silence. He glanced up at her with his red swollen eyes as Marie blew out a long simple breath. The room fell soundless. Frank was afraid to move and for a long while, he could not. Frozen in place, he gazed at his wife. His legs felt like they were one hundred pounds each and finally he ascended to his feet. His hands shook and his mouth ran dry. Reaching across Marie's body, he closed her sparkling blue eyes. Behind him stood Grace as unmovable as her father. She had been awoken by a voice. A voice that spoke her name, a voice she thought sounded like her mother's. She followed it to her parent's room, only to find her father crying at the bedside. Grace wanted to cry too; she wanted to, so badly, but could not. She tried to force tears to her eyes, yet it was useless. The two of them both stood there in quietness. Grace spotted the bible next to her mother's bed. Moving from her paralyzed spot, she picked it up and clutched it to her chest. She squeezed the bible; remembered all the memories she had had with her mother. At last, tears rushed down her face as Grace ran to her room. All Frank could do was to watch his daughter in astonishment. He felt as though something had pierced his body. Burying his face in his hands, he wavered a bit and almost fell backward. Sweat glistened on his forehead as he refocused his mind. He had phone calls to make, but didn't want Grace to hear.

Grace lay curled up in her bed with the bible in her arms. Tears dripped from her face onto the cover of the leather bound book. She sat up and looked at the book. In a moment of rage, she threw the bible onto bedroom floor. She felt abandoned by God. She was so faithful to him and all she wanted was her mother back to her. A small white envelope flew out from the pages and lay separate from the bible on the floor. She had never seen it before. Wiping the wetness from her face, she hopped out of bed and picked up the envelope. On the front of it, the word *Princess* was printed.

Frank retreated to the basement of his home. In the dank darkness, he fumbled for the light switch. Finding it, he slumped down in an armchair that was close by. He found the phone, dialed a number and waited for an answer. He could not sit still; hence, he had to get up and walk around. In his movement, Frank bumped a side table and knocked over a framed picture. The picture fell onto the cement floor and cracked the frame's glass. He cursed loudly and froze caught in the moment; he stared down at a picture of himself and Marie. Suddenly, he broke down in tears he couldn't stop himself. The other line of the phone answered and Frank could barely speak. Finally, clearing his throat he gave the details of his wife to them. He finished the conversation, hung up the phone and headed toward the back of the basement. Locating a small fridge, he removed one half-a-bottle liquor from it and opened the bottle.

Back in Grace's room, she sat in the middle of her floor. She carefully tore open the envelope to reveal a small folded pink piece of paper. Sliding out along with the note was a small chain necklace with a silver cross.

Grace read the letter she had found. It was hand written and addressed to her, it read:

Dear Grace,

My darling daughter, please do not be afraid. I love you so much and will always love you no matter what. Live in the faith that I have taught you and know that Jesus will always be there for you. I am giving you my cross necklace so you will remember that I will always forever be in your heart.

Love,
Your Mother

Grace turned to her mirror and put on the silver cross necklace. She cherished it with all her heart. The memory of her mother was interrupted by a loud yell of Grace's name. Jumping from her spot, she flew out of her room and into the den.

A large man sat in a leather chair wearing black sweat pants and a white shirt. Wrinkles and a pair of thin glasses surrounded his face. The man had not shaved for two days and he was losing his hair. He held a remote control in his hand flipping the channels of the TV as fast as he could.

"What's the matter Dad?" She asked a bit out of breath.

"I can't find my damn show!" He huffed back at her.

"Well, it's Friday and your show only comes on Mondays."

"Oh...well...what the hell time is it? I'm hungry, fix me some lunch."

"Ok Dad ok."

Grace went into the kitchen, took a couple of deep breath and closed her eyes.

Please Lord let me have patience with him.

She made a quick sandwich for her father, then returned into the den and handed it to him. He lowered his glasses and broke his gaze from the TV screen.

"What's in it?" He barked taking a good look over the sandwich.

"Turkey and cheese with mustard on wheat bread. Just the way you like."

"Mustard! I don't like mustard, you dumb girl! I never eat mustard."

With that, he knocked the plate out of her hands and spilled the sandwich onto the carpet.

"Go make me another one and this time with no mustard on it!"

He went back to watching the TV as Grace bent down and picked up pieces of the fallen sandwich.

"Dad, did you take your pills today?"

"Pills? I don't take any pills and where is my sandwich?"

Grace returned to the kitchen and removed a pill container from the cabinet. She checked the label and then counted out two small white pills. She gathered a new sandwich again with mustard and a glass of water.

"Here take these please."

She presented the pills and the glass of water. He gave her a scowl and grabbed the pills from her swallowing them down with the water.

"Here is your sandwich."

He took another look at Grace with cruelty and bit into the sandwich. He chewed his food while he mumbled at her about the correction of the sandwich. Grace knew the man very well and that mustard went with just about anything her father ate.

"Dad, when Ruth gets here, I am going into work. Ok?"

The man scrunched his face as he swallowed food, ignoring her almost completely.

"I will have Ruth lay out some clothes for you when she gets here."

The man stuffed more of the sandwich in his mouth as he turned up the volume on the television.

"I won't be home until five o'clock, ok?"

She looked hopelessly at her father as he handed her the empty plate the sandwich had been on. The man slouched a bit more in his chair and flipped some channels as if Grace was not even there next to him. Again, she went to the kitchen and gently put the dish in the sink. Back in her room, Grace finished applying her makeup and slipped on her shoes. The doorbell rang and Grace's father yelled at her to answer it. She grabbed her purse and her red binder and answered the door. A short woman stood at the entrance, fixing her golden curly hair from the wind and rain. Grace opened the door and led her inside. The woman was covered in a white shirt and pants and wore a nametag that bore her name, Ruth. She was in her mid fifties, yet wore large amounts of make up to hide the fact. The make up did its job well, but the half-framed glasses that sat on her nose didn't. She squinted at Grace and brandished a friendly smile.

"Whew, it sure is a mess out there." The woman stated as she wiped her feet.

Grace closed the door behind them and took Ruth's coat. Again, a yell for Grace came from the den that could barely be heard over the volume of the TV. They both glanced toward the direction of the noise.

"How is he doing today?" Ruth asked.

After hanging up Ruth's coat in the foyer closet, Grace turned and answered.

"Oh, he is doing ok, he forgot his pills again."

Ruth gave her a worried look.

"And how are you doing dear?"

"Good, I'm feeling strong today." Grace replied.

A second howl for Grace came from the old man then a painful cough afterward.

"Well, dear it looks like I had better get to work. You get going now; I don't want to hold you up."

"Thank you so much Ruth, I'll be back around the usual time."

With that, Grace removed her own coat from the closet and went out through the front door into the rain.

The rain poured down on the front windshield of Grace's green truck. The window wipers barely did anything to clear her view of the road. As she struggled to see her way, she mumbled soft words of prayer for a safe journey to work. Grace worked at the local church and school named St. Luke's; there, she was part of a Christian out reach program. On Mondays and Wednesdays of each week, Grace taught a religion class for teens of ages twelve to eighteen. The class was made up of about twenty or so students. The teens that made up the class were ones that attends either a public school that did not teach a religion class or school dropouts. The outreach program was the idea of the pastor at St. Luke's. He was known for his strong community work and had a reputation of being a Good Samaritan.

Grace loved to teach her class; although most students did not attend every week, Grace put her heart into the class. The salary was poor, yet Grace did not mind; the commission she was paid was more than enough.

She enjoyed her class more than the pay and the students were good kids who didn't cause a lot of trouble. Yet, teaching the class was Grace's second love, her first was working as a volunteer adult leader for St. Luke's youth group.

The youth group was called Life In Faith Together, or as the teens called it LIFT, for short. Every Sunday night, teens from the surrounding area schools would gather and learn about topics that affected their lives, giving talks on scriptures, and how Jesus influences their lives. Not to mention the food that was served and activities that were conducted; not only was LIFT a place to for Jesus' influence in the teen's lives, but it gave them a place to hang out with others and take a break from their home lives.

Along with two other girls, a middle aged man, and a priest, the five of them would gather together and plan out LIFT's upcoming events and activities. The two other women of the adult group were both married, unlike Grace. Martha and Kathy were like the two sisters Grace never had. They were both older than Grace, but Martha was the eldest of the three. Always giving their advice to Grace about womanhood and not to mention the latest gossip around the church. The two women would continuously be trying to set Grace up with someone from the church. But, when it came to points of view on the candidate, they often clashed for various reasons. Grace had never taken up a date with any of the men she was matched with, except one.

Mr. Nelson Fithet, this is the one man that Martha and Kathy actually agreed upon. Grace never really saw what the girls liked about him. Grace found Nelson to be repulsing and self involved. He used church on Sundays for his personal use, to pick up single women instead of worshiping. The date Grace shared with him was purely to humor her friends, then to find a relationship of any sorts. Grace had always been more involved with her class and youth group to have time to start any kind of a relationship with anyone. Nelson was new to the community and was just getting settled into the church. He would constantly hound Grace and her friends about joining LIFT. Martha and Kathy agreed on his enrollment to the group, but Grace thought otherwise. Nelson's reasons for joining were not

Christ-centered and he's rarely connected with any of the teens.

The truck barreled down the highway as Grace turned onto the exit ramp into the city. Grace had always enjoyed the country rather than busyness of the city. Yet, Grace had lived in the city before. For ten years, Grace stayed with her mother's parents after her death. Grace's father had taken a difficult road after his wife's death. His grief was consumed by alcohol and he became a very heavy drinker. Frank would often lash out at Grace and hurt her physically and emotionally. Fearing for her safety, Marie's parents pulled Grace from her childhood home and placed her into a new setting, giving her a new outlook on life.

Though she intensely loved her father, she knew this was for the best. While living in the city, Grace discovered that finding God in her life was harder. This was a difficult time for Grace; her faith was tested, pushed, and almost lost during high school in the city. She learned how God was absent in most of her classmates lives. Her senior year was the most difficult, with news of her father's failed liver transplant and how he suffered through two strokes.

Shortly after high school, Grace moved back to the country to take care of her father. Vowing to return to the city and put Christ in teen's lives, she attended a community college for two years. Grace took night classes and gained her associates degree in education. During the summer of her second year of college, Grace dreamed up the idea of LIFT.

St. Luke's Church wasn't too far, once in the city. Traffic was heavy in the city as Grace cautiously maneuvered herself through it. Rain kept pouring down as she passed two policemen, car lights flashing, inspecting a car that had slid into lamppost. Grace took in the vision and asked God for his strength to be with those who may have been injured. Grace turned her eyes back to the road and could see her church up ahead.

The red and grey-bricked building was fairly new and did not take long to build. The church was small in size, yet every Sunday it seemed it became more crowded with each passing week. Grace loved the church and although it's square and a bit dull in external appearance, it's inside shone with beauty. Grace pulled her green vehicle into an open spot in the parking lot. Grabbing her red binder and purse, she stepped down into the flooded parking lot. She used her binder as cover from the rain that poured down on her. She made her way to the side entrance of the building and quickly entered.

The warm air inside the complex tingled Grace's skin as she shook off her wet binder. Although it was a short distance from her truck into the church, Grace's clothes were drenched.

"You seem to be a little wet miss." Commented a man.

Grace brushed back her hair and looked up to face him. The man that stood in front of Grace gave her half-unsure smile. She glanced over the man and quickly recognized him. Eugene Miff was a man in his early forties he wore a maroon polo shirt that was tucked into tan pants that sat high on the waist. His unshaven face and tired eyes looked at Grace with eagerness to see her.

"Hi Eugene, it's really coming down out there." She replied wiping the rain off herself.

"I am glad you made it here safely Grace." He told her.

Eugene was a gentle man always willing to do a good deed or lend a helping hand. He joined the LIFT youth group after hearing about its lack of adult leaders. He had been single his whole life, never having a relationship of any kind. Living this way his entire life made things easier for him, he would say. His simple touch on the group worked in many ways and brought quite a different appeal to them. Eugene was good at helping the newest teens enter LIFT, not pressuring them or forcing them to do anything. Most of the guys gave him a hard time about being single, but liked Eugene because he was the only male leader in the group they could really connect with.

"Is everyone else here yet?" Grace questioned.
"Uh, yeah and a visitor too." He answered as they both walked down a side hallway to the conference room.
"Who's the visitor?" Before Eugene could answer, Grace saw him with her own eyes.

It was Nelson Fithet. He sat with one leg crossed on top of the other, slouched in his chair with Martha and Kathy on either side of him. The two girls seemed to be dripping over Nelson's every word as he spoke. He suddenly noticed Grace when she entered the room and immediately shot up in his seat.

"Well, Grace you seem a little wet. Is it raining or something outside?" He asked followed instantly with an appalling snicker.

Nelson was dressed in a deep white button down shirt that was loosed at the top, which sat un-tucked over his faded blue jeans. His dark hair was positioned perfectly with a gallon of hair spray - no doubt, as his matching dark eyes searched her up and down.

Grace pleasantly sat down in her chair opposite Nelson and gave a swift glance at both women. Martha and Kathy stared back at Grace with bright eyes and dazzling smiles smeared across both their faces. Eugene placed himself next to Grace and observed the tension between the two groups.

Grace sat motionless as Nelson's dimpled smile flashed at her, waiting for an answer to his ridiculous question.
"Hi, Nelson. It's funny to see you here I thought you might be out making sure the bank didn't float away with all this rain." Grace snipped to him.

Nelson gave her back a playful smirk.

"Well, the girls here asked me if I wanted to sit in on your little get together today and I happily accepted."

"Have you asked Father Warren yet?" Asked Grace.

"No, he is out right now making a run to the soup kitchen." Kathy said.

Grace glanced again at both of the women on both sides of Nelson. She then opened her mouth to give another remark back to them, but before she could, Eugene interjected by clearing his throat loudly.

"Ok then nice to have you here Mr. Fithet." Eugene said.

"You can call me Nelson." He interrupted.

"Ok...um...We are a youth group centered on God and his church and every Sunday we..."

"He knows about LIFT, Eugene." Martha stated.

"No it's ok." Nelson smiled. "Please continue Eugene."

"No, don't continue Eugene, you should not be here Nelson." Grace finally said.

"We need him Grace, for the weekend retreat." Kathy added.

Grace huffed back in her chair and thought to herself.

"Eugene, really, continue tell Nelson what we do on Sundays."

"Well, we give talks, read scripture, or act out skits. Sometimes we play games or just hang out."

"That sounds great." Nelson said smiling at Grace again.

"Oh and we usually serve food and drinks too." Eugene mentioned.

The room was quiet for a moment and Eugene again cleared his throat. Grace breathed out a sigh and looked around at everyone.

"Speaking of food, I'm hungry." Eugene noted. "Where's the pizza?"

"I haven't made an order yet. I was waiting till everyone got here." Martha said.

"Well, I would like green olives if you don't mind, Martha." Eugene stated.

Martha scribbled down his order as if she had already known the request. Yet, she looked on with worried eyes toward Grace. Grace had her face covered by her hands. She seemed to be in deep prayer. She ran her fingers over her silver cross necklace. Finally, she looked up at everyone once again and then closed her eyes.

"I have to apologize to everyone. I have been very frustrated lately with myself. I don't seem to concentrate on my faith. With everything around me recently, I don't know why I am having so much trouble." She opened her eyes and locked them on the two girls. They looked back at her with compassion.

"Is it your dad Grace?" Kathy asked. Grace shook her head in agreement.

"Not only that, but I feel as though there is something missing from my life." She added.

"Sorry again that I was short with everyone early, we have a big weekend coming up and I am really looking forward to it. Let me go and pick up lunch for us and then we will finish up preparation for this retreat." Grace now smiling at everybody took a deep breath and stood up from her seat.

"You wanted green olives Eugene right, anything else?" Eugene was quiet for a moment then Nelson quickly cut in saying.

"I would like ham on it...if that's ok with you Eugene." Eugene approved with giving a nod.

"I will get a veggie style for us girls." Kathy and Martha smiled back at Grace as she left the room.

Grace stopped short in the hallway back toward the parking lot.

"Was that you again mom? I know you watch over me. Grace whispered to herself. Thank you for reminding me of how I should act out of love."

Grace opened the outside door to the parking lot and quickly spotted her beat up green truck and sprinted toward it. Wiping rain from herself, she started the vehicle and left the parking lot.

She took caution driving in the rain because the road was slippery. Traffic seemed to be heavier than usual.

Grace looked ahead of herself and noticed that at the intersection, there had been an accident. Police and fire trucks surrounded the area. Through the rain, it was difficult to see in front of her. As she passed the scene,

Grace turned her head and struggled to focus on the accident in order to understand what had happened. She noticed three cars had run into each other. Broken glass and metal were all over the street. She gasped at the wreckage and immediately started praying for the victims.

"Oh merciful Lord I pray that you may surround those people in your love. Help the emergency workers use the skills you have given them at their best. Watch over all who are driving today that they can get to where they are going safely."

Grace returned her view back to the road ahead of her; just as she did, she saw that the car in front of her was at a complete stop. She let her foot off the gas and slammed hard on her break with both of her feet, and the tires screeched in the rain. Jerking the steering wheel to the left, she tried to miss the car. It wasn't enough; the right side of her truck struck the other vehicle, scrapping the tail end left side of it. Grace's truck stopped finally half way onto the cement median.

Grace noticed that she had come to a stop and opened her eyes. Looking up she stared straight at the vehicle she had just hit; it was a red mustang.

3

The air outside became strangely warm as James stepped out of his beloved vehicle. There he stood, simply astonished at what had just happened. A twelve-inch green scar was left imprinted on the backend of his mustang. He closed his eyes and then opened them again wishing the mark would be gone. Walking over to the spot, he hunched down to take a closer look. He ran his fingers over the cut in almost disbelief that it even happened. James barely took a glance at the other vehicle that had hit as he still examined his car. James shut his eyes once more this time anger got the best of him.

Why me and why now...I don't need this.

Finally, James turned to the other vehicle in rage. Standing to his feet, he clenched his fists hard and moved quickly to the truck.

This guy is going to get it.

He thought to himself as he charged in the vehicle's direction. But, before he made it to the truck, out stepped Grace from the passenger side door.

James's eyes locked on her with captivation.

At that moment the rain stopped.

James was caught dead in his tracks.

"Oh my goodness...are you ok?" Grace asked.

"I'm a..." James sputtered.

He could hardly get his words out. Turning around, as if Grace had been talking to someone behind him, he faced his car. James looked again at the huge green scar made on his vehicle. He blinked his eyes and remembering his anger burst out,

"NO, I'm not! Do you see what you have done?" Whipping around toward Grace now.

"This car is a classic; I can't believe you would be so careless!"

"I am so sorry." Grace returned calmly. "I will pay for all of the damage."

"You're right you will pay for it!" James demanded pointing his finger at her.

"I want all your personal information right now!"

Grace suddenly shocked noticed she had left her purse in the truck. She head back to get it. By now, since James' mustang was still in the street blocking traffic, quite a few vehicles had lined up behind it. A man sitting in a silver BMW honked and shouted at them at the same time. James glanced over his shoulder at the growing crowd of impatient cars.

"Hurry up, would you?" James called to Grace as she returned with her purse.

She fumbled it around digging through it for her license. The purse slipped a bit and fell out of her arms dumping the contents onto the road. A few laughs could be heard behind them as the line grew.

"Oh, come on." James sputtered, rolling his eyes and throwing his arms in the air. Grace bent down and started retrieving her things. Shaking his head in frustration, James began to help her. He picked up her checkbook, a set of keys, and a small case of makeup. A small business card slipped out from between the checkbook; the one

Grace used to keep in contact with the parents at the church. James picked it up and read it. The card had the church name on it and a few phone numbers where Grace could be reached.

I am late for work and I get fired and I am late to lunch which gets me in a wreck with some church girl.

He returned her items back to her. She looked into his eyes and gave a small thanks.

"Here is my license." Grace said handing it to James as he exchanged it for his.

"Do you have a pen?" He asked.

Grace reached into her purse and gave him one. James started to scribble down her information on the back of her business card. Nevertheless, before he could finish, a loud horn blared in his ears. He looked up at the man in the BMW as he yelled at James.

"HEY, move that piece of junk buddy!"

James became a bit nervous as he noticed a police car heading toward them.

I do not need that. He thought.

Shoving the identity, pen, and card into his pocket, he pointed toward Grace trying to tell the BMW driver that it was her fault. Unsuccessfully, James gave the man a quick salute in mockery. More honking insinuated and louder voices could now be heard.

"I will contact you as soon as I get an estimate." James hollered to Grace.

She nodded back to him in approval. Trotting to his mustang, he fired up the engine and slammed the door. Claps and a few cheers could be heard behind him as he sped off, leaving Grace behind.

*　　　*　　　*

James sat in the parking lot of Mario's Italian Restaurant.

What just happened? He thought.

James entered the restaurant and was ushered to a table. The man, who had already been seated, sat with his back to James. The top of the man's head was covered in dark hair and was balding a bit, but not a gray hair in sight. As he approached, James noticed that man wore a sharp clean suit. Then James came face to face with the man and he noticed a dark and trimmed goatee on his face.

James met him with a smile saying.
"Thomas, how are you?"

Light blue eyes looked back at James and Thomas answered.

"Good, good have a seat James."
He took a seat opposite Thomas at the table.

"Good to see you could make it."

"Sorry I'm late I-"
Thomas held up a hand cutting him off.

"No need to explain, I'm just glad that you could get away from work and meet me for lunch. I know how busy you are."

James avoided his uncle's eyes and looked over the menu.

He glanced up at his uncle as he reviewed the menu. The man looked very well. James couldn't tell his very successful uncle that he had just lost his job. Thomas had worked very hard raising James and being a CEO of his own company at the same time. Thomas had always done his best trying to give James the most of his time. Yet, at times was not there for him and he knew it. He was proud of James for pushing past the pain of losing his parents and being able to be independent. Thomas had a hard time with his brother's passing away and his own new life that he was thrown into. James couldn't let the man down.

The waitress came over and took both of their orders. Thomas leaned back and took a deep breath.

"When I got your call, I have to tell you that I was shocked. We haven't talked in a while."

James played with his cloth napkin, still trying to avoid his uncle's face.

"I've been pretty busy lately; we have been getting close to finishing some accounts with some big clients. But, what about you, how are you doing?"

Thomas flashed a shy smile and shifted in his seat.
"Well, since you asked." He paused to gather a bit of breath.

"James, I am getting married."

He quit playing with his cloth napkin and now looked his uncle straight in the eyes. A small silence passed and finally James stuttered out.

"Congratulations. Wow...I mean...that is great news Thomas."

Thomas coyly shot another smile and began to laugh mildly. James joined him in laughing at the awkwardness.

"I have been meaning to tell you about her...I mean Jan, her name is Jan. I wanted to get your blessing before we really tie the knot."

James was stunned that he wanted his blessing. He hadn't talked with Thomas face-to-face for at least a month or longer.

"I can't wait for you to meet her. She is so great."
"This is wonderful, when is the wedding going to be?"

"Well, we wanted to wait till the weather warmed up a bit so it won't be until next spring."

James had never seen Thomas like this. Usually he was all business and corporate. Treating everything like a board meeting, but this was as if he was a different person.

How could one single person change another person's life this much?

"Ok, so Thomas Mason is getting married." James quickly said.

The waitress came back to their table with their food. She seemed to linger when giving James his meal and ever so slightly gave him playful glance. Thomas picked up on this and after she had left the table asked James.

"So, what about you, any lucky lady in your life?"

James was surprised at the question, but didn't let it show. He had never really thought about it that much. Work seemed to always come first in his life. James was glad for Thomas was just confused at this possibility even for himself.

"Nobody, really." He answered honestly taking a bite of food.

"I am sure Jan knows some people, that is, if you were ever interested." Thomas offered.

The last thing that I want is to set up on a blind date.

"Oh no that's ok, I think I can manage." James strangely answered.

Manage! I can't even manage to hold a job how do I ever expect to manage a love life.

The two went on about their lunch talking about more work, sports, news, and Jan. James all the while never mentioned the fact that he was unemployed. When the waitress came back and cleared the finished plates, she left the bill on the table.

"I'll get it James, my treat." Thomas said wiping his mouth.

"No, allow me Thomas, as a little engagement gift to you and Jan." James quickly said grabbing it.

He fished out his wallet and retrieved a credit card handing it to the waitress. She took it with a smile and hopped away with it. They talked a little while more, and then the waitress returned with a swallow look on her face.

"I am sorry sir, but I am going to need a driver's license to verify identification of the card." She asked to James.

He pulled out the licenses from his pocket and gave it to her asking,

"Is there a problem with the card?"

She looked at the license and back at James comparing it with the credit card.

"I am sorry, but the card was denied credit and by our policy we have to check the owner's license."

James was bewildered at the card's denial and even more, he was stunned at the next thing the waitress said.

"And if your name is really Grace Connelly then this credit card is not yours."

4

Grace pulled into the church parking lot. She carried the pizzas in her arms when she entered the meeting room. Everyone still sat in his or her places, papers and notebooks scattered all over the table. They looked up at her when she came in. Kathy was the first to ask.

"Where have you been Grace?"

Grace had been gone for two hours. After the accident with the red mustang, she had to get her truck pulled out of the median. The truck was beaten up, but still started. She picked up the pizzas and then got stuck in traffic a bit when returning to the church.

She plopped down in a chair and buried her face in her hands. Martha rounded the table to her and comforted her.

"What happened, my dear?"

Taking a deep breath, she wiped back her hair and cleaned her face. She told the group of the accident and the guy she had dealt with. It just seemed to hit her now the whole experience of the situation.

"Are you alright?" Eugene asked.

"Yes, it just happened all so quickly." She replied.

"Well, it's over now Grace, and if you need me to drive you home I would be glad too." Offered Nelson.

"Thank you all, but I am ok. I just need moment to clean up and then we can get back to planning this weekend."

She left the room and the others talked amongst themselves about Grace.

"The poor girl, it's bad enough that her father is sick, can't she just get a break." Martha said.

Kathy agreed with her and shook her head in disappointment.

"This guy deserves some payback." Nelson acknowledged.

Eugene seemed to perk up and said.

"Listen, let's just make this retreat weekend the best ever. We all know how much she loves the teens and LIFT. She needs this it will raise her spirits and get her mind away from everything."

They all agreed to help make the weekend a great one not only for the teens, but for Grace too. When Grace returned to them, they all got right to work, planning.

5

Thomas had taken care of the restaurant bill and the two of them now stood in the parking lot as James explained the giant green scar on his father's car to his uncle. As Thomas bent down to examine the damage on the mustang, James stared at Grace's driver license in his hand.

"You're going to have to return it." Thomas said implying the license.

What a waste of time that is going to be.

"Yeah, I know." James replied silently.

This day has been disaster.

"Listen I have to get back to work, as you do. It was really good to see you James I am glad we did this."

Thomas pulled out his car keys and turned to his own vehicle.

Still staring at the license, James finally broke his trance and looked up from it toward Thomas.

"Right, it was good to see you to Thomas and congratulations again." He shouted to him.

"Hey, if you need anything James, don't hesitate to give me a call."

Right there James wanted to tell his uncle about his job, his loneliness, and his anger. His pride held his mouth shut and he gave Thomas a short wave.

Thomas sat in his office, a giant picture window sat behind him drawing out the downtown buildings that were around him. The room was neatly furnished with expensive furniture and black and white photos of skyscrapers in silver frames hung on the walls. It was even rare to find him in his office; usually he is either in a production meeting or attending a managing seminar. Today, he is reviewing the annual budget from the east coast branch. His office phone beeped and he looked over his dark framed half reading glasses at the caller ID. It was his secretary Carol; he pushed the intercom button and spoke.

"Go ahead Carol."

Carol's very warm and crisp voice came back saying,

"Sorry to bother you Mr. Mason, but your fiancé is on line three."

A smile wrinkled across his face.

"Thank you Carol, I'll go ahead and take it."

Carol clicked off and Thomas hit line three and picked up the receiver on his phone. His large leather chair rubbed together as he leaned back in it.

"Hi, honey what's up."

"Sorry to call you at work, I just wanted to know how it went with James during lunch. I know how excited you were to tell him the news."

"It went great, he seemed to be doing very well at Kruger and the news went over wonderful." Thomas removed his half glasses from his face and tossed them on his desk.

"Oh that is good to hear dear, I can't wait to meet him."

"I was thinking about that actually, how would you feel if all three of us went out to dinner next week?"

"That would be wonderful; I will make arrangements at Crystal Lake for us."

"Sound good sweetheart, I'll see you tonight."

"Bye"

They both hung up their phones and Thomas flipped through his phone number list and found Kruger and Sons. He dialed the number waiting on the line. A squeaky voice came over the other end and introduced herself as Peggy.

"Hello may I speak with James Mason please."

A short silence went by and Peggy cleared her squeaky throat.

"I am sorry, but Mr. Mason, doesn't... uh work here anymore." She said tripping over her words.

Thomas was astonished at the news.

Had James lied to me about his job?

His forehead crinkled at the thought. Peggy cleared her throat once more with another squeak and asked Thomas if he needed anything else. He replied that he didn't and hung up the phone.

He was now confused about James and worried for him. He was unsure what to do. Dinner with James might make him uncomfortable and he wanted to help James in anyway that he could. He also didn't want to point out to him that he had lied and disappointed Thomas in the process.

It had been a half an hour and James was sitting in his car in parking lot of Kruger and Sons.

What is happening? How have I lost everything? What have I done to deserve this? Who can I turn to?

The thought of calling Thomas and telling him everything crossed his mind. Thomas could easily get James a job at his company, maybe not in his field, but job nonetheless. James didn't want to hang off his uncle for the rest of his life. Yet, again, James didn't know what he wanted out of life. He knew success was something gained through experience and hard work, Thomas had taught him that. But, something was missing for his life. A career, house, wife, children maybe, something was not there. James felt empty and completely alone.

Dragging back to his condo once again for the second time that day, James had no idea of what had happened to his life.

The next day came around and James awoke feeling nauseous. The night before he had struggled with himself, his mind wouldn't let him rest. Questions filled his head, he felt lost and anxious going through most of the night without sleep. He now sat in front of his computer staring at his resume. He entered the ending of employment date next Kruger and Sons Inc. under the employment history section. He leaned back and blew out a breath while running his hand through his hair. The computer clock read one thirty. He hadn't even taken a shower yet and it was the middle of the afternoon.

A knock rapped on his door and he was caught off guard almost tipping out of his chair. Quickly grabbing his bathrobe he threw it on and then went to the peek hole to check whom it was. James recognized the visitor. It was his landlord, Burt. Through the peek hole, the view distorted the man on the other side. He wore his thinning hair to the side in a bad comb over and dark thick mustache covered his mouth. Overweight and seemed to be sweating, he wore several gold rings on his fingers. His tanned body was a bad contrast to the dark red shirt he wore over black pants. Burt knocked a second time now and James jerked the door open. Holding his bathrobe with one hand and the door in the other James greeted the man.

"Burt hey what's up?"

Burt glanced at James up and down. A confused look came over the short man.

"Ah, Mr. Mason am I bothering you right now?"

"No oh um...no your not. What can I do for you?"

"I have come to collect rent from you. I haven't received it in the mail yet this month, and I wanted to make sure you were alright."

James gave the man a sideways look and answered him.

"Oh I am sorry I been so busy this week with work and all." James lied.

Truth was that James was coming up short on his budget this month and was waiting for his next check from Kruger. He took a moment and thought about how he was going to get his final check from the company. He settled on the fact they would probably send it in the mail.

"Let me go and get you a check right now."

James let the round man in his condo and padded back to his bedroom. Burt stood in the living room waiting for James' return. He took a look around the place. The couch was draped in thrown clothing and the wide screen TV was on but seemed to be muted because there was no sound. Papers and documents were spread out on the square dinning table as a garbage can next to the table was overflowing with trash. He could see dishes piled up in the kitchen sink and open boxes of snacks and drinks sat on the counter. Burt was staring into the kitchen when James came back to him. He noticed the landlord's direction of vision and asked.

"Burt may I offer you something to drink?"

"No, no Mr. Mason I'm quite alright, if you could just give the check, I'd be on my way."

James handed him a check for three-fourths of the rent. The rest he gave the man in cash. James always had an emergency stash on of money on hand in case he ever needed it. Burt shoved the payment into his pockets and turned to leave.

"Thank you sir." He said taking one last look around. "And if there is ever anything you need you have my number."

James thanked him for coming and showed him out, locking the door behind him. Now looking around at the condo himself, James noticed the huge mess and once again read the clock. He sucked in air and said aloud.
"At least it's Saturday."

Grace had been up since seven a.m.; today was her cleaning day. She did laundry, changed bed sheets, dusted, swept, disinfected, and did yard work, all before noon. Although she was not alone, the home nurse Ruth helped her. She mostly helped care for her father while Grace took care of all the rest. After taking a shower and changing her clothes, Grace served lunch for Ruth and her father. Ruth took her seat at the table after helping Frank into his own. The old man scooped up his napkin and tucked it into the collar of his shirt ready to eat. Grace sat down on the table with a mixed bowl of fruit and took her own chair. She looked at Ruth and gave a smile and then to her father who was scowling at her.

"Let's eat." He barked.
"Dad, we have to say prayers first." Grace reminded him.
"Prayers are for the weak." He shot back to her.
She gave him a concerned look. He curled his lips in disgust and bowed his head. The two women did likewise.
"Dear Lord, You have given us such a bounty of goodness and strength, yet I know we fail day in and day out. Help us to return to You when we need you most. Bless us O'Lord with Your love and compassion. Let us always know that You gave us Your beloved Son, Jesus to help with our walk toward You and through our lives."
Grace opened her eyes and lifted her head with a smile as did Ruth.

"That was very nice dear."

"Thank you."

Grace looked toward her father, but he was too busy wolfing down food to notice. She sighed in frustration and began to eat.

After the meal, Ruth and Grace cleaned up the table, while Frank watched TV. Ruth handed Grace the dishes while she washed and cleaned them in the sink.

"So, how are you holding up dear?" Ruth asked passing her more dirty dishes.

"It seems everybody has been asking that lately."

"Well, there are a lot of people who are worried about you."

"I am just fine, but Dad is not." She set some clean dishes in a drying rack.

"He has really gotten bad in the last few months. I...really am blessed with you coming over to help during the day." Grace let the water out of the sink and grabbed a towel to dry her hands.

"You've been here with him during the day haven't you noticed his decline?"

Ruth returned the last of the plates to the cupboard and turned to Grace.

"Yes, but he mostly sleeps and watches television." She now had tears in her eyes as she took Grace's hands in hers.

"Oh Grace, I am just afraid he'll have another stroke or...or something worse. It would be unbearable for you."

Grace now had tears in her eyes as well.

"The Lord has given this duty to me Ruth and whether it's hard, frustrating, or unwanted. It is mine."

"Well, I'm just glad you have got this weekend coming up." Ruth said wiping the tears away with a tissue.

"You look forward to this every year."

"I don't know what I would do if I didn't have the church or LIFT in my life."

"I made all the arrangements at the Charter Home for that weekend. It will be no trouble at all."

"Thank you so very much Ruth, you truly are an angel."

The two embraced and Ruth whispered into Grace's ear.

"Your mother would be proud of you."

6

James fumbled with his keys trying to open his condo door, his arms were full of Chinese food and he was trying to talk on his cell phone. Finally opening the door, he stumbled in and dropped the bags on his new cleaned kitchen counter top. He scrambled toward his computer and sat down in front of it.

"No, no I wasn't fired." James lied. "I was just let go. I guess there were cutbacks or something."
The person on the other line talked a bit, asking questions.

"Well, I am up to date on all the latest software expansions and I have experience in live updates and transfers." James explained.

"I can start anytime."
The man talked more.
"Right." James answered.
There was a long pause and James stood to pace.
"Uh huh, I'm still here." James listened.
James's face dropped and he leaned his arm on the wall closest to him. He hung his head and bit his lower lip.

"I understand."
"Well, I'll keep in touch Dr. Smith."
"Yes."
"Thank You."

James hung up the phone and tossed it on the dinning table. He sighed with a deep breath grabbing the bag of Chinese Food. Dr. Smith had been a professor in college that James thought might have an apprenticeship position open. It was full and would not be open until at least next year.

Of course because I just can't get a break.

James chewed on some rice while he thought of the next phone call he could make. He walked to his fridge, opened the large door and searched for something to drink.

Why does God hate me? Am I doomed to have nothing in life? Where are you God and why don't you help me?

James slammed the fridge door in frustration. There on the front of the door, stuck with a magnet was Grace's driver license.

He stared at it a bit and then ripped it from its place. Sitting back down to the table, he pondered a moment, shoving sweet and sour chicken in his mouth.

I have no way of getting in touch with the girl. How am I supposed to find her?

Eating more chicken and rice, James read over the license.

I could just mail it to her and be done with it. Or I find her name and address in the phone book and call her.
Just then, he remembered the business card he had taken from her.

I'm sure that has her number on it.

He flipped out his wallet and hunted through it. As he searched, he noticed something odd.

Oh no.

James realized that his license was missing from his wallet.

We must have exchanged licenses and never returned them to each other. Wait. Did I give her mine? Did it fall out of my wallet?

There was only one way to find out.

He found the business card and read it over. The card had her name and under it was her title of religion class teacher and LIFT youth group adult leader. Grace also had a home number and church number printed on the card. At the bottom read J M 4 6.

I can't call her at home. Can I? I did tell her I would get in touch with her about the damage. What am I supposed to say?

James decided to call the church number and ask for her. He dialed it into his cell phone and froze before he punched the send button.

This is all her fault.

He tapped the send button and listened to the rings. On the third ring a click on the other end picked up.

"St. Luke's Church, this is LuAnn how may I direct your call?" asked an elderly female voice.

"Hello, I'm looking for a-"James looked down at the license. "a Grace Connelly that works there."

"Oh our Grace is wonderful, isn't she? She is such a sweet girl and so humble."

"Um, yes, but I just need to speak with her."

"Oh, are you a parent of a child in the religion class?"

"No, I'm a just trying to get a hold of her to speak with about-"James thought quickly. "About the youth group."

"The youth group, well, I can answer anything you want to know about the youth group." LuAnn answered proudly.

"I would just really like to talk with her if that-"He was cut off by LuAnn.

"The youth group was started by Grace and Father Warren a few years back and has thrived ever since, though I am sorry to say that the need of adult leaders is lacking, but that doesn't stop Grace. She jumps right in every week and they all have wonderful time."

"That's very nice." James said rolling his eyes. "Do you think I could talk to her now?"

"Oh she is so busy lately with the class and all, oh and plus her poor father failing in health." LuAnn went on talking.

James started to become annoyed.

I don't have time for this old bag.

He became very stern saying,

"If you could please just stop babbling and let me speak with Grace herself that would be wonderful."

LuAnn was sharply quiet for a moment. James thought she might have hung up on him. Then lightly clearing her throat said.

"I am sorry sir, but Ms. Connelly is not in today. Thank you for calling St. Luke's our daily masses are six am and eight am Monday thru Friday. Our Sunday Vigil mass is on Saturday at six pm and services for Sunday are at six, nine, noon, and at six in the evening followed by Living In Faith Together. Good day sir and God bless." With that, the woman hung up on James.

He closed his phone shut and shook his head.

Ok now what am I suppose to do? I am not calling her at home. I'm sure LuAnn is calling her right now to tell her about some strange man was calling for her. I never know who will answer at her home, possibly her husband or somebody ready to chew my head off. That will get me nowhere.

James sat at his table, eating his cold food thinking out a plan. Flipping the business card in his fingers, he pondered the meaning behind the two letters J M and numbers 4 and 6.

Stupid Christians, always trying to do good and spread "the word", but in the end just end up with nothing.

James' faith was lost after his parent's death. Before then he had been to church and even went through Sunday Bible school. His parents said that since they never had the chance, he should. But, how could a God that truly loved life and family destroy a young boy's life? James wiped the thoughts from his head and decided on a second idea of getting his license back.

7

St. Luke's was a church located within a decent neighborhood in the suburbs of the city. It was built in the early 1940's, long before the neighborhood that surrounded it was even thought of. The adjoining school was constructed twenty years later after the boom of the city's growth. The pale color of gray granite and dark bricks gave it a gothic taste, a tall steeple reaching to the heavens looked over its inhabitants. Though the church's design was dated, that didn't stop the community from attending it. The number of patrons grew every year; however the church was grossly under-funded, but money never kept the doors from opening and the man who was responsible for them each day was more than a saint.

Father Robert Warren, a priest of the Franciscan order, was one of the main reasons parishioners came each week. A well-fit sixty-year-old man was a credit to his cause and dearly loved by his parish. Not only did his sermons each Sunday have historical and biblical reference, but were tightly wrapped around the questions and problems of today's world. Father Warren wasn't only known for his words, his actions often spoke louder than them. One parishioner was over-heard once saying that Father Warren would drive his car around the city just looking to do good deeds. Between soup kitchens, mission trips, and charity events, he still impressively had time for his priestly duties. Visiting the sick, hearing confessions, and he even held a monthly chastity discussion group for young couples. For the LIFT youth group, Father Warren was pinnacle. He very much wanted to be involved in the lives of teens. Father Warren was a huge inspiration to her faith, so when Grace came to the good man with her idea for the group and upon describing it to him, he couldn't help but embrace the young girl full of joy. LIFT had been a hit ever since. Even though St. Luke's and Father Warren gave out so much, never asked for anything in return, sadly got less than that. Yet, the Shepherd never quit on his flock and Father Warren wasn't about to start either; besides, today was Sunday and he had a job to do. It was just before the six o'clock evening service and Father Warren found Grace readying herself for the mass.

Sunlight shone through the stain glass window next to Grace. Rainbows of color poured down on her as she adjusted a microphone stand and laid out sheet music in the band section next to the front alter. The gentle priest stepped out of the sacristy fully clothed in his service garments with a grin spread across his face. He caught Grace's eye and gave her a wink and broader smile. Grace returned the smile and brought both of her hands to her face cupping them around her eyes like binoculars. The priest squinted at her animation, looking confused then quickly reached into his side pocket and produced a thick pair of glasses, setting them on his face. His eyes were instantly enlarged behind them and Grace was now in better focus. He tipped an imaginary hat to her and walked to the back of the church readying himself and greeting fellow worshipers just as the service began.

The red mustang came to a halt at the far end of the church parking lot. James killed the ignition and sat back in his seat. He eyed the old brick building, thinking to himself.

I can't believe I am doing this; she had better be in here.

Evening was approaching and the sun was beginning to set. The lights from inside the church could be seen brightly shining through.

This parking lot is almost full. It's amazing this many people attend this place.

James looked at his watch. The six o'clock evening service was almost over.

He removed Grace's license from his inside coat pocket. He looked at her picture. She was smiling sweetly, her blonde hair tucked behind her.

How am I going to approach her? He thought.

What am I going to say?

Maybe she has been trying to get in contact with me.

I guess I did tell her to call me about the insurance from the accident.

I could just wait for her to call me then. Forget even going into the church. That's what I'll do.

He started the engine and waited a second, pondering the idea of leaving. James scanned the parking lot searching for a decision. Then he saw it, the busted-up green pile of junk that had disfigured his mustang.

Oh, no way.

He began to get upset remembering what had happened. He could see flicks of red paint where she had hit his car. Disgusted now, James jerked out his keys and stepped out of the car slamming the door shut. The cool outside air blew over his face as he made his way to the front entrance of the church.

Two huge wooden doors were propped open and he could see the inside of the brightly lit church. James could hear music coming from inside as he approached, a joyous song, an uplifting tune. Now, as he stepped over the threshold, he felt like he was being drawn in. As if the music and the warm glowing lights were beckoning to him. Moving through a small foyer, James looked ahead and he could bearably see the front alter. The church didn't seem so crowded until he had made it this far. People filled every pew and the back and sidewalls. The music was louder now, a song he thinks he had heard before. A couple of men, possibly his age, eyed him as he stepped closer. James looked up now just realizing the ceiling seemed to go up forever. Shining metal chandlers hung from the ceiling radiant with light. Stain glass windows covered the adjacent walls and some of the front, but they were dark now because the sun had gone down. More and more people, James could see above him, in a balcony bellowing out the hymn along with the others. They seemed to be packed in as tightly as they could. All focused on the music and as a whole.

One of the men beside James tapped his shoulder passing him a dark green hardbound book open to about the middle. James took it without question and the man moved from his spot in the last pew and offered it to James. Almost as if he knew James would be arriving, he had been holding this place for him. James didn't recognize the man, but gave up on placing him and put his attention back to the front again. For the first time he noticed choir on the left side of the front alter. It was made up of seven people all singing with their hearts content.

There on the end of the choir stood Grace. She looked more different than James could remember. Maybe it was the lighting or the surroundings. All of a sudden, he felt nervous about approaching her face to face. He replayed the car accident in his mind. He recalls blowing her off and speeding away from the scene. Leaving her alone.

A wave of heat came over James. Nausea set in. It happened quickly. The people around him seemed like they were right on top of him, crowding his personal space. His breathing sped up. His vision became blurred. The singing voices turned to muffles and slurs. Not making any sense. James had to get out. Get some air and clear his head. His legs wouldn't move they felt like cement blocks. Sweat droplets spotted his forehead. He refocused a bit trying to control his breathing. It didn't help. The song was coming to an end. The green hardbound book he had been holding felt like a thousand pounds, his arm muscles tensing from the weight. Sweat now drenched his face as his body wavered out of control.

He knew he was going down. It couldn't be stopped. The song was done and someone was saying something. Mumbles was all he could hear. Panic came over him as his mind race around thoughts.

What would happen? How would people react? Would Grace see him or had she already seen him? Did she recognize him? Oh, this is going to be a real attention getter!

It was his last thought, James's brain came to blank.

Just as if someone had shut off the lights, James blacked out. Heading down fast, falling to his left toward the open main aisle that led to the front of the alter.

The green book beat him to the floor first with a loud echoing pound slamming against the wood floor. Next came James smacking his head on the end of the pew on the way down with the top half of his torso laying in the main aisle and the rest in his pew.

8

Grace had thought Father Warren's sermon was wonderful. It had a nice message and she was thinking she might use some of his points in one of her religion classes. Grace enjoyed sitting up front in the choir, even though she wasn't a great singer, she loved to lift her voice to the Lord. The church seemed more crowded than usual this night. If only they could get more funding, the church could maybe get a face-lift and possibly the school would be able to expand. Only with God's grace would that happen. She said a small prayer on the subject.

Father Warren was returning to the alter table from finishing Holy Communion. Grace cherished having a close up view of the holy sacraments and procedures of the mass. The reenactment of Christ's Last Supper into the service was her favorite. What would it have been like to be there in the company of Jesus Christ?

I wonder if He had a choir singing praises at his Last Supper. She thought.

Now she needed to prepare for the next song. The choir was made up of seven singers including her. Martha and Kathy were both members as were other church members. Grace gathered up her folder and opened it to the correct page. She really didn't need the words to the song, but liked to have them out just in case someone else needed them. The song began and Grace explored the congregation, most of them joining in the song. She still couldn't believe the full house tonight. People lined the sidewalls and back of the church. The balcony looked like it was going to explode because it was so full. She was thrilled at the thought of so many Christians attending Sunday services. The happiness made her voice raised even louder in praise. She smiled at a young girl in the first row who held an oversized green book in her small hands singing along with the music. The little girl reminded her of herself at that age, though Grace didn't make it to church every Sunday. She sure did her best then. Her mother loved to attend and until she got sick, Grace would sit just as that girl was in the first pew, watching her mother sing in the choir. The memory gave Grace hope for someday she longed for, that children of her own will follow her footprints and love the Lord as she did. As the song was coming close to the end, Grace now noticed, also in the first row, Nelson. He stood belting out the words to the song. But she was sure; no doubt that he didn't mean them. He was too busy eyeing a woman across the main aisle from where he was. The woman didn't seem to even perceive his eyeballs ready to pop right out of his head.

Grace was disgusted at the display.

Why couldn't he just focus on the mass for five minutes? Maybe if he would make an effort and not be so egotistical...

She stopped her thoughts and finished the song as it ended.

Father Warren stood at his microphone, raising his hands into the air placing a blessing over the people. Grace's eyes jumped back to Nelson for just a moment. She was met with those bulging eyes on her. He gave a slow wink. She quickly looked away and back at Father.

What was that? What was he trying to say?

Grace began to get upset at Nelson's cockiness. The priest asked for a moment of silence for those who had passed away that week. Grace settled her thoughts and prayed. But the thoughts of Nelson were still there. She shouldn't think so cruel of him. He wasn't even her type, but who else was there?

A loud boom sounded through out the church stillness that made Grace jump. She opened her eyes and looked up to see someone lying on the ground in the middle of the main aisle. She squinted and covered her mouth slightly in astonishment.

It couldn't be him, could it?

9

The red mustang zoomed down the highway with James at the wheel. His destination in front of him, but as he roared toward it, it kept getting further away. Desert surrounded him as far as he could see, barren, flat, and dry. A shimmering figure rose off the highway, dressed in black, arms stretched to the sky, waving vigorously at the mustang. The man in black stared James down with jumbo-sized eyes as he sped by. James whipped his head around following the man when he passed. His arms now drooped at his side as he disappeared into the dust kicked up from car. All of a sudden, horns screamed into James' ears. He returned his vision to the road ahead of him. Out of nowhere, a green truck came tearing onto the highway directly at him. James jerked the wheel left, but the car swerved right instead. He compensated swinging the wheel the opposite direction just as another green truck came steaming his way. Dust swirled around him as he tried to return to the blacktop. A police car, sirens blaring, popped up in the rear mirror chasing James down. James quickly applied the brake to slowdown, but it only resulted in acceleration. He slammed the brake with both feet and the mustang took off climbing in speed, growing ever distant from his end. More green trucks come from everywhere trying wildly to hit him. Unexpectedly in the passenger seat next to him appeared J. R. Kruger. James was taken off guard by the man. He glared James straight in the face, his after-shave burning James' nostrils. Kruger reached passed James and opened the driver side door.

James looked in horror as the highway could be seen speeding underneath outside the car. Kruger got in James' face saying.

"Your fired, Mason get out!"

With one last look at his ex-boss, a wrinkly smile on his face, he pushed James from the car.

"NO!" James shouted.

His eyes shot open coming face to face with two giant pair of eyes looking down on him.

James now recognized the thick glasses and trimmed mustache, all he could say was;

"you..." pointing at the older man.

Then blacked out a second time.

10

It couldn't be him. Could it?

Grace thought as she strode down the main aisle to get a better look at the man who had passed out and slammed his head on the end of the pew.

Why is he here?

Has he come to embarrass and humiliate me here too?

Father Warren had quickly ended mass and had someone, a doctor, she thought checking the man's head and vitals. The doctor, or EMT someone had said, or whoever, had concluded that the man would be fine. But guaranteed he would have quite the headache when he woke up and calling 911 would be unnecessary. The EMT, offered to stay around until the man came around to double check him and make sure that he felt ok before he left.

Serves him right, a good whack on the head.

Grace calm down. Whispered a voice.

She blew out a resentful breath and spotted Martha, who was buzzing around clearing the church of onlookers and giving the man some space. Grace was now close enough to him to take a better look. He looked different to her, probably because he wasn't yelling at her. He was more handsome than she remembers even though he had drool on the side of his mouth.

"Grace, Grace!" Kathy came walking quickly up to her. Grace turned from the man, thinking she didn't even know his name.

"Hey, Kath, what's up?" Grace asked trying to seem uninterested in the attractive guy who lay at her feet.

"Well, the youth group has gathered in the basement and it's just me and Eugene. And he's having trouble starting the grill."

Grace had almost completely forgotten. LIFT was supposed to start right after the service was over. How could she have disregarded it so easily? She blamed the unconscious man that she wanted to kick.

Whoa, Grace take it easy - Came the voice again. Relax.

"Ok." Grace said recollecting herself. "Get with Martha and help her see out the rest of these people. Then find Nelson and I'll meet up with you both down there in...," she thought a minute glancing around the church. Her eyes found Nelson, his arm propped up against a wall; he was leaning over a young woman with red hair. The two laughed, probably at one of his lame jokes.

Who was she? Grace pondered.

Oh, no way! I am not jealous.

She closed her eyes sagging on her shoulders.

"Grace?" Kathy asked. "Are you ok?" She too had also seen Nelson's antics.

"Listen I'll go pry Nelson away and you send Martha down after she is done playing traffic control."

"Ok sounds good." I'll stay here with this guy until he wakes up and then send him on his way.

She also wanted to give him a piece of her mind.

"That won't be necessary." Came a voice from behind them.

Father Warren came walking up from outside the entrance of the church. Now, in his solid black priest attire.

"I will stay with him until he is safely ready to leave and the doctor here checks him out one last time."
Grace opened her mouth to speak, but Kathy cut in saying.

"Sounds great Father." She then motioned to Martha who was ushering out the last concerned couple from the church. She assured them that everything would be fine. Grace was a bit thrown off by Father Warren's interjection. But then again all her emotions seem a tad off tonight. She took one last look at the man and joined the others on their way downstairs.

"So, Father," asked the EMT, "This ever happen before."

Father Warren clasped his hands behind his back searching his memory looking up to the ceiling and turned to the EMT.

"No, most of the time I just put them to sleep."
The EMT chuckled at the comment.
Just then, the young man started to wake up.

11

James blinked as the light burned his eyes. The EMT held James' eye open checking his pupils.

"You seem to be fine." The EMT observed. "No concussion, that's good."

James shook his head and a pounding set in just above his left eye.

"Do you have a headache?" The EMT asked.

"Um..." James eyed the priest who stood to his left that leaned in, listening to the conversation. "Yeah, I do."

"Well, I would suggest you take a couple of aspirin and get some ice for that bump." The EMT said pointing at James' now red spot on the side of his face.

James gave the spot a rub and more pain shot through his skull.

"Can you stand?"

"I think." James answered.

Still looking at Father Warren, James grabbed hold of the pew in front of him and hosted himself up.

"What about hallucinations?" James asked the EMT who was returning his medical supplies to a small bag.

"Huh? Uh, well are you having some?" He turned back to James.

James rested his hand on his injury rubbing it again and closed his eyes. He opened them again one after the other. The priest still stood motionless, respectful.

"No, I guess not."

"Good, well Father I believe he will be ok to drive home."

Something clicked in James's head.

That's it, I didn't stop to help the priest and God had me fired from my job. I knew there was a connection some how.

The priest thanked the EMT for his assistance and showed him out of the church. James was alone in the church. It was quieter then he thought it would have been, having been full of singing worshipers only moments before. Rubbing his head again, he winced in pain.

How could this happen? This is just my luck. I guess God has a nasty sense of irony.

"I am sorry I didn't get your name." Father Warren had returned walking toward James.

"It's James Mason."

James now for sure knew that this was the man he had passed up on the interstate. The man who stood soaked in the rain, who had simply asked James for help. How hard would have it been to have given assistance? To take time out for those who were in need?

James hung his head with a heavy heart.

"It's nice to meet you James. I'm Father Warren, pastor of this church."

They shook hands; the priest's felt warmly inviting as if all it ever wanted to do was to comfort.

They released each other's hands.

"Father, you may not remember, but..." James started.

"I remember, I maybe old, but my memory is still intact." He said tapping finger to his temple.

"I just want to say that it was a horrible day for me that day."

"Don't worry my boy, I understand. Said the priest a smile grew on his face. "You didn't need to come all the way here to tell me you had a bad day. But I admire your humbleness and forgive you."

James's heart leapt in his chest.

He returned with a small smirk to the priest in appreciation.

"Actually," James pulled out Grace's driver license. "I really didn't come here for you."

Father Warren took the license and examined it. Returning it and nodding said.

"I see, follow me."

He led James to the back of the church to a small side stairwell that descended to the basement.

The priest turned back to James. "And we'll see if I can find some aspirin and some ice for that bump."

12

The aroma of grilled hotdogs filled the air. Blaring music was being played from some corner of the room. A young girl ran between Father Warren and James followed closely by another girl then a third, who carried a plastic cup of some kind of dark liquid. James guessed it was soda, given the fact that the three looked to only be in their teens. The room was small which made it very crowded. Two six-foot long tables sat in the middle of the room. Both spotted with teens seated in various places. Some were stuffing hotdogs in their mouths, others are talking to one another very loudly compensating for their equally if not louder opponent, the rock music. James felt a light breeze hit him; an oversized outer door could be seen across the room that led outside. Through that door, outside, floodlights lit up the night showed more teens and what seemed like volleyball net. Also, through the open door a black grill, the source of the fresh hotdog smell smoked away, a man about James' age stood behind it.

Father Warren walked up to another smaller table that held various other types of food and drinks. He tapped someone on the shoulder who had his back to them. The man turned around to face them and Father Warren introduced James to the man.

"Hello." The man said returning a ketchup bottle to the table and rubbed his now free hand on his shirt, stretching it out to James.

"I'm Eugene."

James took the man's hand looking him over. The thinning hair and wrinkles under his eyes told James that

"Eugene" was at least forty years old. The wrinkled polo shirt, now with a fresh ketchup stain, and kinaki pants gave him the appearance that he had slept in his clothes.

James smiled at Eugene as he jammed part of his hotdog into his mouth. Though it was hard to understand him over the music, talking with his mouth full made it worse.

Somehow, James understood him when he offered James a hotdog. A tin foil pan held about half a dozen burnt hotdogs. James concluded they must have been Eugene's handy work and he politely declined. He wasn't at the least bit hungry, he just wanted to get in and out.

The music was intensifying his already pounding headache. Father Warren put together his own hotdog asking Eugene where they might find Grace. Eugene explained he had last seen her in the kitchen. Father thanked Eugene and he and James continued.

Before they made it through the kitchen door, out came Kathy, arms full of two-liter soda bottles. She just almost ran into the two men, almost dropping the bottles.

Regaining her balance, she set them on the table next to her. A few boys ran up and refilled their plastic cups praising the woman, explaining they had been dying of thirst. She gave them a sweet smile turning that smile toward Father Warren and James. She introduced herself to James, and he returned the gesture. She asked him about his head and if he was feeling ok. Or so he thought she did. The music that was playing seemed to have gotten louder. James deciphered her words and gave a thumbs-up. Even though the blasting music was killing his head, Father pressed on into the kitchen James followed.

Finally, the rock music was slightly muted as they entered the room. James breathed a sigh of relief. The kitchen was small and looked old, another woman who looked as though she had been up all night moved through out. She didn't notice the men. She was well distracted with emptying a fresh bag of chips into a bowl. A cell phone held snug to her ear as she bounced around.

"No, I told them they were to go straight to bed." She said opening a bag of pretzels. "Don't argue with me, we've been through this before."

A hopeless expression came across her face. She continued to talk as she opened the door to a white fridge. The door blocked the men's view of her; all they could hear was her frustrated voice. James didn't see Grace around and his head was aching, he didn't want to be here any longer. He just wanted to go home and rest. The woman closed the fridge door saying.

"That's impossible I never said that!"

Anger in her voice could clearly be seen in her face, and then she spotted the two men who had been waiting and watching her. She gave both of them a small wave with a free hand. The priest mouthed Grace's name slowly to the woman. She lifted the phone from her ear, a loud voice could be heard on the other end, but James couldn't make out any of the words. She told them Grace had gone outside. She returned to the phone argument with who James presumed was her husband.

Back out into the main room that now sounded like a live concert, Eugene was on his knees wiping up a spilled drink and Kathy could be seen moving some chairs around as they made their way to the back door exit.

Grey smoke came off a sizzling grill to the right. More teens ran through the night some laughing others playing volleyball, a group of boys tossed a football back and forth. The music was considerably quieter out here and some pressure seemed to be relieved from James' head.

His attention was turned now to the man who had been standing behind the grill. Dressed in a flashy silver dress shirt and black pants, a white apron draped over his clothes and he held metal tongs in his hand. The man looked up from his grilling when he heard Father call his name. James didn't catch the name because his ears were still ringing from the music inside. The man beamed a perfect smile teeth whiter than white. He reached out, awaiting James' hand; James saw his cue and gripped the man's hand introducing himself.

"James Mason."

"Nice to meet you, Nelson Fithet."

"I thought Eugene was grilling tonight." Asked Father.

Nelson snapped the tongs a couple of times answering with a smug smile.

"Oh, he was, until he almost caught himself on fire and burned most of them. I then took over; I put him on spill duty. He is better at that anyway."

He snapped the tongs a few more times and flashed another pearly smile.

Kathy came out of the back door and walked up to Father Warren, who was finishing his hotdog, and told him that they were almost ready for him. Father excused himself from the two men and returned inside with Kathy.

Nelson turned back to James facing him.

"So Jimmy, which one of these kids are yours?"

James was shocked at the question and put off by Nelson's casualness toward him. Nobody called him "Jimmy"; he detested it.

"Actually, none of them. I'm just here to see Grace Connelly."

James said with all seriousness.

Nelson raised his eyebrows as his mind wandered the possibilities, finally saying,

"Well, you've come to the right place, Jimmy." Nelson speared a piece of meat. "Hotdog?"

13

Eugene was bent over the grill, rapidly clicking the ignite button. Nothing happened. A tinfoil tray of burnt and crispy hotdogs sat next to him.

"Everything ok over here?"

Eugene looked up from his work and saw Grace on the other side of the grill. She had noticed that Eugene seemed stumped with the grill and walked over to help.

"Well...no, everything was going fine until the flames went out. I can't seem to get it restarted."

Grace gave a look of support, but had no idea what to do. She grabbed the tin of hotdogs.

"Hey, these look great."

"Oh, thanks." Eugene replied. "I just wish I could get this thing going."

The man looked determined. That is what Grace respected most about Eugene. He was dedicated, reliable, and genuine.

"You're out of gas." Came a voice.

Nelson strutted up next to Grace and pointed to the gas tank.

"Whoa, what happened to those?" Nelson asked indicating Eugene's dark hotdogs.

"They are fine, I'm taking them inside." Grace shot back in defense. Nelson rolled his eyes.

"I think that there is an extra gas tank in the utility shed. I'll go get it." Eugene offered.

"Actually buddy, someone spilled something inside and they need you to clean it up." Nelson said patting Eugene on the back.

"I'll get the gas tank and take over on the grill."

Eugene nodded removing his white apron and handing it to Nelson. Grace tried to protest, but Eugene took the tray from her hands and went inside. She watched him as he shuffled away.

"That was completely rude!" She said turning to Nelson. He was tying the apron around his body.

"Hey, I'm just trying to help out." He returned picking up the metal tongs next to him.

"If Eugene can't be the man to handle this job then let him stand aside and let a real one in."

Grace was enraged.

"Even if you were half the man Eugene is, you never-- "Grace stopped short, controlled herself and turned from Nelson.

He shrugged his shoulders and adjusted his sleeves.

"Who wants hotdogs?" He announced snapping the tongs together with flair.

The weather was reasonably warm outside and Grace was glad that the kids could play in it. She was still angry with Nelson and his lack of respect for Eugene at the moment.

What a jerk. She thought. *He's not fit to help out with LIFT.*

Grace stopped her thoughts. When has she ever been the one to judge? She heard her mother's voice again reminding her; it's not her place to determine who's Christian enough and who is not. With God, everyone gets an equal change. That settled it; she quit thinking about Nelson and put it in God's hands. He would take care of it.

Grace watched the teens play, chasing each other, laughing, not a care in the world right now. Whatever their home life was like, here they could forget the hurt, sorrow, and pain.

She closed her eyes in prayer.

God, thank you for their care free attitudes, being able to be themselves here, and giving me the opportunity to connect You to them. Help me to have patience and an open heart to any you may be leading me to. For me to know Your way is good and use my life to represent that.

Grace opened her eyes feeling renewed. Yet, looking straight ahead, her heart sank once more. The guy she couldn't seem to get away from. He was talking to Nelson.

Getting along with each other no doubt.

He was probably here to collect payment from the accident.

She was actually surprised to see him down here, figuring he would have just gone home after he awoke. Grace was sure Father Warren had a hand in it. Always the shepherd looking for the lost, wayward sheep out there, herding it home.

How did he find her anyway? She had never seen him at church before, why now? Who was this guy anyway?

She pondered these thoughts as she drifted his way.

14

Nelson kept talking to James, something about saving bonds and such. The conversation didn't keep James' attention. He was surrounded by teens that played on carelessly. They didn't seem to have a worry in the world. Smiling faces jumping, giggling, and relaxed. It made him want to jump right in on the fun. James had never had that as a teen growing up, the freedom to get away from it all. Not that his uncle was a bad parent. Thomas just wasn't in the position to be a father. It all happened so fast. How do you tell a corporate partner that you had to cancel a budget meeting because your nephew wanted to go to a baseball game, or visit the zoo? James loved his uncle, but it was hard to love as father. He felt he had to prove his worth to his uncle. Thomas disapproved of James' juvenile activities, treating him more as an adult than son.

Having been raised without many friends, it was hard for James to connect with the kids of his own age. He never built forts in the woods or watched cartoons all day long, instead he learned the ways of a corporate empire. Thomas had built a multi-million dollar financial firm, which conducted accounts worldwide. Therefore, when the rest of the neighborhood was out riding bikes, James was learning the basic requirements of good office management. When he finally went off to college and was expected to succeed, it didn't come easy. It seemed all the other students were motivated for a degree that they had chosen, something that they sought after for a career. Going into a business major wasn't what James wanted. The problem was that he truly didn't know what he wanted to do. He wanted something fulfilling, yet his heart was confused. Above all, he wanted to make his uncle proud. He finished school with a bachelor's degree in marketing. Thomas approved of James' accomplishment and James felt respected and valued. From then on, all James strived for was excelling for approval from his uncle or his employer, boosting his social status and self-image.

Now as footballs flew through the air and chasing ensued. James couldn't help but want to interact. Where was this feeling coming from? He had seen kids playing before and not felt this way. Why now? He scanned the crowd of young people; whoever was in charge here had their hands full, then his eyes caught sight of her. Grace broke out from behind a small group of girls coming his way. Her natural beauty stunned him again. Sparkling blue eyes locked on him, her blonde hair lightly flowed around her perfect face. He moved from his spot closing the distance between them.

Suddenly his mind panicked. He hadn't thought of what he was going to say to her. His mind raced through possibilities, he wanted to impress her but had no plan whatsoever. Unprepared and entranced by her, James almost didn't see two boys who ran in front of him oblivious to his presence. Taking a step back to make room for them to pass, he came inches from colliding. Before he knew it, he was face to face with Grace. She crossed her arms in front of her. James swallowed searching for words to say. His head pounded as if working against him. Just leave, he thought. Forget the whole thing. Turn and go now. Finally, she spoke saying.

"Red mustang, right?"

His mind swirled with thoughts, his memory clicked into place.

A bit of a smile came to his face.

"Yeah, you remembered!"

"Well, of course I do. You hurt me. Yelled at me, publicly humiliating me, and then sped off leaving me in your dust." Grace said now with anger in her attractive face. James was caught off guard by her statement. He looked away from her and shoved his hands into his pockets.

"Furthermore, I don't know why you are here. You are not welcome." Grace was more upset than he could expect. "What, have you come to humiliate me again?"

She looked aside casting her gaze off in the distance. James could see she was furious with him. Why should she be? He was not in the wrong. Was he? It didn't matter, she was the one who had hit him.

"Hey!" He shouted back now clearly angry as well.

"You are the one who hit my car. You owe me."

Their argument was now considerably louder than they intended. A few teens looked at them. A small group who had been playing volleyball left returning inside.

Grace noticed and felt ashamed of her words and actions. This was a safe haven for these kids. Half of them probably had parents who fought like this at home. They didn't need to hear it here too. She took a deep breath calming down. James had seen everyone's reaction too.

What was happening? This wasn't his motive for coming here. He felt irresponsible. Just then, he remembered.

He removed his hands from his pockets, holding Grace's driver license.

"Um, here." He said returning the identity to her.
She looked down at it. Bewilderment spread across her face.

"How did you get this?" She asked taking it in her hands.

"We must have switched them during the accident. I guess I was too caught up in the moment and more worried about the damage to my car that I didn't notice."

James realized she was right. How could he have been so inconsiderate? He was overcome with regret.

"Grace." He softly said.

Immediately she looked him straight in the eyes. They shined back at her. She saw something working inside of him.

"I'm sorry. Sorry for being insensitive that day and for treating you the way that I did." He admitted.

Calmness came over Grace.

"I forgive you." She returned a smile now on her face. "I am sorry too, for damaging your car."

Looking at her amazing eyes James said something he never thought he would.

"Don't worry about it."

Grace was wide-eyed as he continued.

"It's no harm done, just a scratch, you don't have to pay for anything."

What was he saying? It was his dead father's car. A classic. However, that didn't seem to matter to James. He felt something he never had before.

Relaxed, contented, he couldn't describe it.

Grace thanked him again. The man who she had hit earlier that week was not the same who stood in front of her now. He had changed and she knew what it was that was working inside of him. She wanted to know more about him. For heaven's sake, she didn't even know his name yet.

But, before she could ask him, someone yelled the word "incoming". Grace didn't see it coming. He did. Just inches from her head, he reached out and caught the leather football that was headed for her.

"Whoa." He said palming the ball.

Grace jerked her head back out of the way.

"Be careful guys." He playfully yelled to a group of boys who had let their game get a little out of hand. "Here go long!"

He pulled back and launched the football back at the boys over their heads. They ran after it, howling in astonishment over the toss.

Grace was impressed.

Who is this guy God?

She shot him a sweet smile holding up the driver's license.

"I guess this means I have yours."

He nodded. She looked away biting her lower lip and smiling again.

He enjoyed her smile.

"By the way. I don't even know your name yet." She said feeling childish.

"It's James." He answered

Her heart leapt at the name. She now knew for sure God had his hand in what was happening. James was not what she had expected from their first encounter, but then again God was involved and he always had a plan.

15

Everyone had gathered back inside almost all were sitting on the chairs that formerly surrounded the tables, which are now folded up and set against the wall to make more room. Although James had no intention of staying before, something was different. All he wanted was to return Grace's license and get his own back. Now, he had agreed to stay for the rest of LIFT's evening activities. What those activities were, he was unsure. He didn't like not knowing what was going to happen. It's not what he wanted to do. Yet, he felt compelled to stick around. His new plan was to sit through the night and maybe get to know Grace some more. As he scouted out a seat toward the back of the room, Martha, Kathy, Eugene and Nelson were at the front of the room. James didn't see Grace or Father Warren. He wasn't so sure about this. Maybe he could sneak out, but he couldn't leave without his own license. He would just let Grace get back to him.

No, just forget about her and go get a new license.

Why hadn't he thought of that before?

Ditch her and this place. You need to find a job! His thoughts reminded him.

What will she think when she finds out you're unemployed? You'll look like a fool. Remember what Kruger had said. A fool!

James started to grow impatient.

"Ok, everybody grab your chair and I want you to form five groups of six people creating small circles." Announced Martha, clapping her hands to get their attention.

Obviously, the kids knew what they were doing because they didn't waste anytime with the circles. Some whooped and howled in anticipation of what was about to happen. That was it for James; he was out of here. This was his chance. No one would detect him. He stood from his seat and casually moved toward the door that he knew led to the stairs up to the church and to the parking lot, where his car waited for him. Maybe he could make it back to his condo before it got too late to call around on a few more leads he had for a job. Slowly, he walked toward the stairwell entrance. Cheering himself on as he moved closer to his escape.

"Jimmy, hey Jimmy!" Came a voice from behind him. James knew it was Nelson.

Don't turn around. He thought. *Just keep moving as if you didn't hear him.*

It was too late. James could feel the presence of about thirty pairs of eyes on him. It was nerve racking.

"Yeah, Jimmy come on over here." Shouted Eugene with a huge smile on his face.

Great now he is calling me that too.

James flipped around and faced the crowd of wide eyes and intent looks. He gave a small smirk and wave.

"Here you can sit in our circle." A young dark hair boy offered scooting his chair out to make room.

"Oh, um that's ok I'll just watch." James lied to him.

"Come on James, it'll be fun." Came a sweet voice.

Grace had come out of the kitchen carrying a small sack. James felt something jump inside him at the sight of Grace. He had almost forgotten how attractive he thought she was. Those blue eyes caught his and drew him in. He was powerless.

Fine. He thought, but just for her.

James took the open seat the boy had ready for him and listened to Kathy.

"Ok, most of you have played this game before. But, I'll go over the rules again for those who maybe new." Her eyes rested on James.

"Everyone will go around their circle and pick a fruit for themselves." Grace moved around to each group and handed one person in each circle a huge sock. James wasn't so sure about this. What was this sock filled with?

"Grace is handing out a smacking sock to each circle. The person who receives it must stand in the middle of the circle and call out a name of a fruit. If that is your fruit name then you must call it out and then say someone else's fruit name after it. Then that person must say their fruit name followed by new one." If a fruit is called out and that person replies, but is hit by the sock from the person in the center before they can think of or say a new fruit then that person is in the middle. Does everyone get it?"

A collective "Yeah" came from everyone, but James. He was confused, Grace had handed him the sock and he stood in the center of his little circle. The surrounding faces spread with glee. The teen each sounded off a name of a fruit none of them the same. Then it got to James, he search his mind for a fruit that had not been taken. He couldn't think his mind was blank. Here he was standing in the middle of these teenagers trying to think of name of a fruit that he could be. Banana no that had already been taken, he was tired of be here. He looked off toward the group that Grace was in and she seemed to have been reading his mind. She mouthed a word to him and sprang another one of her tender smiles. He looked back at the eager faces awaiting his choice.

"Mango." James announced proudly looking back at Grace.

The game ensued. It wasn't entirely horrible, James thought as he quickly got someone to take his place in the center. He learned quickly and started to even enjoy himself, laughing along with the others.

After about a good half an hour of playing the icebreaker, everyone lined the chairs back in to rows facing the front of the room again. James found a seat next to Grace as everyone was getting settled.

"So, are you glad you stayed?" Grace asked as he sat down.

James shook his head up and down slowly saying,

"I guess being hit with a giant sock isn't too bad.

But, next time I'll come prepared with a sneaker fruit name that's harder to remember."

Grace laughed. She was glad he had stayed. There was something more to him if she could just break that outer shell. She had seen it when he apologized to her earlier and when he slung the sock around. Maybe he just didn't see it in himself. Father Warren was standing in the front of the room and started to talk. Grace loved to listen to Father's talks. But this was different than one of his sermons. His audience was special and he accommodated them. He also brought a sense of warmth and encouragement to it. Tonight's topic was on our dependence on God. One Grace had heard before, but was excited it was James's first. She hoped that he got as much out of it as she did. Above all though, she wanted to know why God had placed James in her life. She would know all in time.

Father Warren's talk on the dependence on God was a success with the group. The question and answer session that followed had gone longer then they had planned. The night was drawing to an end quickly. Grace now stood at the front of the room and was trying to get everyone's attention.

"Ok, you guys. You all know that next weekend is, the big retreat weekend at Lake Forest so, if you haven't gotten your permission slips in from home yet, I had better have them before Friday." A teen raised his hand and asked for a slip. Grace handed him one. The group started talking amongst themselves getting excited about the trip.

"Hey, guys!" Grace shouted over them. "Also, you have to be here on Saturday morning at six a.m." A couple of groans could be heard and someone asked if they could drive themselves.

"Nope, sorry, but the rules are you ride with the bus or you don't ride at all." She looked around for any more questions.

"Ok, that's about it. Let's end with a prayer and then you guys can go."

The room grew silent as Father Warren led the group in a prayer and gave a blessing to all. Then the teens started helping to clean up, as others caught rides home. Grace spied James carrying a few chairs to the storage closet and quickly joined him.

"Hey, so what did you think?"

James lifted a chair to Eugene who packed it away in the closet with the others.

"Uh, it was nice." He handed off another chair up to Eugene.

James didn't think it was too bad. He just wasn't really interested in the whole religion stuff. To him Father Warren's talk was a bit dry and boring. Hanging around for some food and a game wasn't a problem, but this isn't his sort of thing.

He had better things to do. Grace must have known what he was thinking.

"All first timers have that feeling."

"I'm sorry?" James said.

"Don't worry." She said coolly. "God has unlimited patience and He'll find a way to connect with you."

"What?" James was confused.

Grace gave a cute smile.

"Ok, then what's His phone number, I've been meaning to get some almighty questions answered?" James said pretending to talk on an imaginary phone.

Grace laughed at his animation.

"All you have is faith and the understanding of the life that He has chosen for you."

James was intrigued, where she was going with this.

"Listen, you heard about the retreat weekend right?"

James nodded his head.

"We're going to need all the help we can get. We are going to have quite an attendance."
James knew what she was going to ask.

"I would like to invite you to come along and be an adult leader. Are you interested?"

It wasn't that James wasn't interested, he just didn't want to get stuck watching a bunch of teenagers roam free and out of control all weekend, although this might be a good chance for him to get to know Grace better.

"Trust me." She said. "It will be fun and I'll save you a prime spot on the bus."

"How do I know I can trust you?" He asked with a coy smile on his face.

"You can't, but you can trust God."

CHAPTER

16

It was already Wednesday, Thomas couldn't believe it. He stood in front of his large picture window in his office, overlooking the city. He craned his neck closer to the glass. With the cuff of his shirt, he wiped a smudge from the polished glass. Thomas had been trying all week long to get a hold of James. But, James hadn't answered his phone call for almost three days now. Thomas was getting worried about him. He hoped James was okay. He knew James looked up to him, and thought they might not be on the best of terms, he did love him. When James graduated from college, Thomas was so proud of him. He immediately offered James a position within his company. He wanted to reward James for his hard work. But, James wouldn't have it, he declined the position telling his uncle he wanted to earn a position himself and work his way up. Thomas knew this all to well, he admired his enthusiasm and work ethic, James reminded him of himself. He also respected James' answer, but always told him that the door would be forever open if he ever wanted a job. Time went on and Thomas remembers how James had a rough start when applying for positions elsewhere. Not too many marketing firms were located in the city. All the same, James kept at it. Painfully Thomas watched his nephew struggle for a job. After six months and no luck and after James had taken a night shift job at a grocery store, Thomas had to step in. He invited James out to dinner one evening and pleaded he take a position with his company. He hated seeing James fight and lose. James still passed up the offer, explaining to Thomas that he wanted to earn it on his own. Thomas was frustrated with James, demanding he take the employment. This didn't help, it just made James as equally upset. Thomas didn't back down though, he went on telling James he was ignorant for declining his recommendation. Obviously hurt by his words, James started going on about how Thomas had always instilled in him that he earned his title and status in his career. Telling him how he had to work hard, learn along the way to become successful. How would he be doing that if he were just handed a high-level position. Furthermore, he told Thomas that he had always been pushed into business and maybe that wasn't what he wanted to do. Surprised by James' outrage, Thomas didn't know what to say next. James then stormed out of the restaurant.

That had been almost a year ago. The two lost their connection and only talked maybe once a month after that. Soon after that, Thomas met Jan and the couple dated for a few months. They seemed to hit it off. Thomas was so happy. Somewhere along that time, Thomas heard that James had been hired on at Kruger and Sons. He wanted to call and congratulate him, but never did. He proposed to Jan and she accepted. He wanted the world to know his joyfulness. Yet, he didn't have anyone to share it with. James had been all he had. Ever since Thomas had met Jan, she had shown him how important family was. Now that he was getting married, he wanted James to be with him on that wonderful day. Their recent meeting for lunch had been the first time Thomas had seen James face-to-face in months. Having James back in his life was more important to him now more than ever.

As he stood pondering if he should call him again, his office door creaked open and a short blonde haired woman poked her head into the clean office. Her voice startled Thomas.

"Excuse me Mr. Mason, but your nephew is on line one." Thomas turned from his window and thanked her as she left.

Finally. He thought.

Thomas had to approach this very carefully. With the knowledge that James had been let go from Kruger was a sensitive matter, and he didn't want to hurt James again. He picked up the phone receiver and waited a moment. Pressing the line one button on his phone, he spoke into the phone saying,

"James, how are you?" He waited for a response.

Nothing.

"Hello?" Thomas' brow arched in confusion. Finally, some heavy breathing and then James' voice could be heard on the other end.

"Yeah, that one." Thomas wasn't sure of what was going on.

"James?"

"Oof, thanks." Came the voice again. "Thomas, hey how's it going?" James seemed like he was winded.

"James are you ok?"

"Me? Yeah I'm fine."

"What are you doing?"

"Buying a sleeping bag."

Thomas was dumbfounded.

"A sleeping bag?"

"Yeah, I'm going on a retreat this weekend with a youth group." James' breathing had returned to normal.

"The guy here at the sports store said this was the best one. Had to get it from the top shelf."

Thomas checked his watch, a Rolex; it was a quarter past one. A sports store? Retreat weekend? Sleeping bag? Thomas was stunned.

James must have noticed the time as well because he said.

"I took a couple of days off work so I could be ready."

Thomas knew it was an outright lie and wanted to call him on it. But, he kept his voice cool and remained focused on the reason for his phone call.

"Sounds great James, listen Jan and I wanted to take you out to dinner, so that you can meet her, our treat."

Thomas flipped open his weekly planner. He scanned the calendar with his finger.

"How does this Friday sound, at seven o'clock? Jan's got it all set up."

Silence.

"I'm sorry Thomas, but I've got to be up early and on time on Saturday. I want to get a full night's rest. It will be a long weekend."

Thomas was hurt, blown off for a retreat weekend. Why in the world was he going on a retreat weekend anyway? Typical James, he always wanted to play and never take responsibility. Blowing out a breath, Thomas tried to calm down. He still had to ask James a very important question. How could he phrase it the right way without turning James off? He thought for a minute, listening to him talk.

"Maybe we can do something next week, when I get back. I really would like to meet Jan."

Thomas wasn't sure what he wanted to say yet.

"Sure, that will be fine." He replied.

"Well, I've have got to be moving, I need to get across town and pick up a couple of two by fours." James said.

Thomas's mind was blown. What would he need a couple of two by fours for a retreat weekend? He was about to ask when James said goodbye and hung up. It happened so quickly; Thomas still had his mouth open ready to talk. He hung up the receiver and slumped down into his leather chair. He still couldn't believe it. James had never been on a camping trip before let alone been outdoors over night by himself. Why now? What was making him do this?

The phone buzzed in his pocket as James made a left turn into the lumberyard's parking lot. He flipped open the cell phone and answered.

"Hey James, I saw that I missed a call from you. What's up? How is everything?"

It was Bart Hampton, his only decent friend from Kruger and Sons. James had the thought to give him a call and ask him if he knew of any advertising openings in the area.

"Um, everything is going good, I guess." James contemplated the purchase of two by fours he was about to make and was still confused about what they were for.   "I was just giving you a call to see if you knew of any tips on advertising positions in the city?"

Bart was quiet for almost a minute and James could hear kids in the background on the other end.

"You know it's funny you called me, I just talked to a buddy of mine, who works for Baxter Advertising, last night and he clued me in on an opening within the company." James listened closer, not believing the words he was hearing.

"He called it a "longshot", but said it would be a job of a lifetime." James couldn't contain his excitement.

"Bart, let me send you my resume and contacts when I get home." Again his friend was quiet on the other end.

"Okay, alright, send them to me and I'll see what I can do. But I am not promising anything James. I'm sure you know Baxter's reputation." James did. Baxter Advertising was one of the largest advertising firms in the world. Getting a position within any part of their company was like winning the world series of baseball, everybody got a gold ring.

"Anything you can do would be great Bart. Thanks so much."

They said goodbye and hung up.

James was excited about the possibility of the career of a lifetime, but didn't want to build himself up for failure. So, he put the thoughts aside. Yet, just the idea of getting the job with Baxter gave him a shiver of delight. All he had to do was make through this retreat. Nothing this weekend would be bigger than this opportunity.

17

Grace was so very excited for this Saturday. She had been looking forward to this weekend for quite sometime. The group had so many great things planned to do. Grace was also glad that James had agreed to come along. Something intrigued her about him, she wasn't sure what, but she wanted to find out. Her green truck drove down a small street leading to a small residential area. Beyond the tiny houses, a building came into view. Although she couldn't wait for tomorrow she couldn't stand putting her Dad in a nursing home during her absence. He didn't seem to mind himself, but Grace always felt guilty, as if he was some kind of nuisance.

A brown faded sign read Charter Home as Grace turned into the parking lot. She parked in an open spot and walked to the entrance. At her left, behind a round counter sat an older woman in dark blue scrubs. The woman's face brightened when she saw Grace coming to the counter.

"Hello, Grace."

"Hi Ellen, how are you?"

Almost everyone knew Grace at Charter Home, because she would often bring the teens from LIFT in for service experience. They would come and visit with the residence and serve them a meal. Everyone loved when they stopped in and had a goodtime.

"I'm just here to see my Dad." Grace said.

"Oh, that's right. Your retreat weekend is this weekend, isn't it?" Ellen said, just realizing. "It looks like you'd be having some nice weather for it."

"Actually it starts tomorrow and goes a half day on Sunday."

"It's Friday already? Wow. Hey the next thing you know I'll be living here instead of working."

Grace chuckled at the comment

"Your Father's down the hall, dear, room one sixteen."

Grace thanked Ellen and went on her way. This is the part Grace hated, seeing her Father like this and telling him she was going to be gone. He never liked it when people left him. Grace didn't either. She could smell the stale stench of sanitizer as she moved down the hall. A woman was walking out of her room dressed in a nightgown and slippers; she stopped Grace grabbing her arm.

"Oh, Ethel, I am so glad you came."

The elderly woman was trying to pull Grace into her room.

"I've been baking all day and I wanted you to try some of my treats." She went on.

Grace felt horrible. This poor woman.

"I'm sorry miss." Grace started, holding her hand in hers. "My name is Grace and I am here to see my Dad, who's just down the hall."

The woman looked crestfallen. Grace's heart sank to the floor. Looking at Grace full of hope asked.

"Where is Ethel?"

Grace didn't know what to say to her.

"Ethel is not here, I'm Grace."

The woman pulled back her hand from Grace's grasp, her face upset. She shuffled over to a rocking chair in the corner of the room and sat looking off into the distance. Grace was overcome by emotion, tears starting to fill her eyes. She turned and left before she let them fall.

Recomposed and ready to face her father, she entered his room. The TV was blaring a sports game as she found her father on his bed, he was asleep. She smiled at the sight. Grace removed her coat and turned down the volume on the TV. The man abruptly woke up staring at Grace.

"Marie?" He asked. Grace was surprised at his assumption; he hadn't called her by her mother's name for years. She controlled her emotion at the thoughts.

"No, Dad it's me Grace." She said sweetly.

"Oh, Grace, I could have sworn you were your mother."

Grace smiled at him. He looked pretty good today, awake and alert. She was thankful because she wanted him to understand what she was about to tell him.

"Ok, Dad, now I've been reminding you all week that I am going to be gone through the weekend. But, I will see you on Monday and you can come home on Tuesday. Remember I have LIFT's retreat weekend?"

The man just kept looking at Grace as if he was seeing through her. She took his hand holding it in hers; it was worn and rough. She rubbed it with her other hand.

"Dad? Did you hear me Dad?"

She looked into her father's eyes. Feelings of heartache came rushing over her. She hated this.

"Where is she?" He asked. Grace didn't quite understand.

"I'm sure she is on her way, isn't she? She's always late, but she'll be here."

"Who Dad? Your nurse?"

"No." He said shaking his head. "Your mother."

Grace was shocked; he had never talked about her mother since her death.

Has he had another stroke? She thought.

"Dad, mom is gone." The man gave a look of innocence.

Grace felt awful telling him. Eyes started to tears again.

"It's ok Dad, she's with Jesus now."

Her father still looked unconvinced.

"That can't be." He said.

Wet tears now slowly rolled down Grace's cheeks. She couldn't do this. Maybe she could cancel the weekend. Or maybe just stay home this weekend.

"I just saw her." He said a smile creasing his face.

Grace was so happy to see her father smile. Whatever he was seeing, he clearly felt it was real.

"You know Dad you're right. She's with us in our heart isn't she?"

The man nodded in agreement. He broke his trace with Grace and noticed the TV was on. His smile turned into a frown.

"Hey, I was watching that." He bit.

Grace closed her eyes and knew her good old Dad was back. She felt better now about the weekend. He was going to be fine. Whatever he had just envisioned, she praised God for it. She knew He and her mother were watching over him.

"Ok, Dad I have to go now, I'll see you when I get back."

The man was quickly pressing the volume control on his remote. Grace felt ok with this. Leaning over him kissed his forehead. She was feeling better now than she did in past times she had left him here. She pulled on her coat and walked to the door.

"Grace." Her father yelled.

She turned and looked at him. He flipped off the TV.

"I love you." He said softly.

Grace's heart pounded with affection and poise.

"I love you too Dad."

She turned and left the room. She felt happier than she had in a long time. Grace wanted to run and skip down the hallway, but she stopped short. Knocking on the door, she waited patiently. An old woman came to the door in a nightgown and slippers.

"I was wondering what you've been baking in here that smelled so good." She asked the woman.

The woman's small features light up on her face and a wide grin on her mouth as she opened the door for Grace.

18

The morning was foggy and brisk. James was a bit chilled as he pulled into St. Luke's parking lot.

Hopefully it will warm up today.

He didn't see the school bus anywhere or anyone else. He must be the first one here. He was an hour earlier than he was supposed to be there. It didn't matter, he was too excited. He could hardly sleep last night. He kept waking up and checking the time and it made him feel like a little kid. Why did he feel this way? He didn't care, he was ready. Glancing around the lot again, he suddenly knew he was in second place. A beat up green truck with a red smear on the front end was parked also. James hopped out of his mustang and ran up to it. He couldn't believe that she had beaten him. He arrived an hour early for goodness sake. How long had she been here? As he came upon her truck, Grace was nowhere to be found. James searched the parking lot; there was no sign of her. Where could she be? His eyes fell on the shadowy stone church, the lights glowed from inside.

Of course. He thought.

James walked to the entrance. The interior looked the same from when he had been there last Sunday. Yet, there was a presence of stillness, a moment of calm about it. Probably because there were no people inside, except for Grace. She sat in the front pew resting her head on her folded hands with eyes shut. James walked swiftly, quietly toward the front. He plopped down next to her saying.

"I can't believe you're sleeping in church."
Grace almost jumped to the ceiling with surprise. She quickly recognized James and smirked punching him in the shoulder.

"What are you doing here so early and for your information I was praying."

"I thought I would get a head-start on everyone, I wanted a good seat on the bus."

"Actually I am glad you are here. About that good seat on the bus, I'm going to have to ask you to give it up."

James was baffled beyond himself. She specially asked him to go along with them on the retreat. Now she was saying he couldn't go? This girl is crazy.

"Wait, what do you mean?" He asked with seriousness in his voice.

"Well, we are going to have a full bus with kids. I asked around earlier last week for some volunteers from school and had three sign up."

"So, you kicked me out? What, am I not Christian enough?"

James threw his arms in the air. Grace shook her head and covered her smiling mouth with her hand.

"No, I never would judge you on being Christian enough or not. And I'm not 'kicking' you out."
Relief came over James. He was really looking forward to this.

"I promised the women from school that they would have a free ride there. We really need them and I don't want to lose your help either. The only thing is that you are going to have to drive your car."

James really didn't mind driving, but he wanted to ride with Grace. Maybe she would ride with him? He didn't dare ask, he didn't want to let her know he was attracted to her. He played it cool.

"Oh, that won't be a problem, but I am going to have to put those two by fours in the bus. They stick out too far for me to drive on the highway."

"Ok that will be fine."

They sat a minute in silence. Light from the rising sun outside made the front alter gleamed. Grace turned to James. He didn't notice her. Affection showed over her features as she looked at him.

"So you want to join me?"

James moved facing Grace.

"Join you in what?"

"Praying."

He held up a hand saying.

"Oh, um that's ok; I'm not much of a prayer. Unless it's bottom of the ninth and my team is down."

Grace understood and returned to her own prayers. James watched her for a moment. She looked peaceful. Something was about her, it wasn't just her beauty, but something she had that James was fascinated by. He was determined to find this out.

They only had ten minutes before the bus left. Everything was packed up as teens ran around the parking lot. They seemed eager to get on the way. Grace too. This weekend was going to be interesting. James had grown to be quite the enigma she hadn't thought he would be. She felt bad making him have to drive himself, she much rather have talk to him some more during the two hour road trip.

Grace hoped that James would get the most he could out of this weekend. She knew he had more potential then he truly knew himself. Quickly she recited a helpful prayer for him, giving God control and to take part in this weekend.

Eugene came running up to her carrying a clipboard in his hands. Someone yelled his name and he turned his head giving a wave to him or her with his free hand. He looked energetic and excited about the trip as well. Eugene was a little out of breath when he reached Grace saying.

"Ok, I got a final head count and I think everyone is here and accounted for."

"Great and is everything loaded into the bus?" She asked.

Eugene looked back at Nelson who was slamming the rear bus door closed. He gave them both a thumbs-up.

Grace was glad that everybody seemed cooperative and helpful, even Nelson.

"It's looking good; I would say we are ready to go." Eugene said.

Grace beamed with a smile. She clapped her hands loud and shouted.

"Ok, everyone board the bus, LIFT is out of here."
It was a mad rush for the bus as teens climbed aboard and settled into their seats.

A light breeze hit Grace giving her goosebumps, but her smile didn't fade because she knew this weekend retreat was going to be outstanding.

19

The fresh smell of pine and open air surrounded James as he stepped from his red Ford Mustang. It was intoxicating for him. He put his hands on his hips, leaning back, his spine cracked in two places. Letting out a breath of air as he straightened, the car ride had made his joints pretty stiff. Ahead of him, a small clean path leads up a short hill to a rustic wooden cabin.

Just like the movies. He thought as he unloaded his bags from his car.

A dark haired boy came running from behind, slapping him on the back as he passed James.

"You'd better hurry up before all the beds get taken, man." The boy was walking backwards up the path toward the cabin as he talked. "Or else you'll be sleeping with the bears!" He then took off full speed up the hill.

James was taken off guard by the boy's eagerness. Either he was telling the truth or just giving the "new" guy a hard time. Whatever the case, James was running late. He had fallen behind the bus when he had to make a quick stop for gas on the way to Lake Forest. Sure that everyone had taken all the good beds by now, James hiked up the trail. Upon getting closer to the cabin, the detail started popping out. From further away, the cabin didn't look half bad. Better than he had expected. Yet, as he pulled open the front door, it fell off its side hinges completely off the whole frame itself.

"Whoa!" James called out catching the door in his arms. He stepped back and caught his balance. Setting the door aside, he took another look at what had just happened and shook his head. He stepped through the threshold and the sight that came upon his eyes made him want to run back to his car and leave that moment.

Before the caravan took off from St. Luke's, everyone was broke up into groups. Each of the nine adults was in charge of four teens. James wasn't so sure about the arrangement, but it was too late to protest about it and he somehow trusted Grace's leadership. The boys all slept in one cabin and the girls in another, of course. But, the scene that was before his eyes now was beyond his conception of the whole outing itself. Boys chased girls, towel paper flew, and some girls were squirting another boy with bottled water. To his left, someone had just climbed out a window and from behind a bunk, something smashed what sounded like glass against the floor. He hoped he was in the girls' cabin, yet the same dark hair boy, who had smacked James on the back, was now somehow completely drenched with water told him otherwise.

"Your, bunk is right over there." The boy pointed to an empty bottom bunk bed closest to the entrance of what James assumed was the bathroom. He couldn't tell because the lighting was so bad within it, someone had unscrewed the light bulb.

James slumped on his shoulders and shuffled to his bed. Taking a deep breath, he seriously considered leaving. How easy would it be? Just to turn around, throw his bags into his car, and return to his warm, comfortable, condominium.

Then what would Grace think?

He certainly wasn't here to be a babysitter. She would understand right? Or she would think he was a quitter, that he couldn't handle these kids and if he was ever going to consider any kind of relationship with her, it would be over. Wait; was he actually interested in this girl? She was attractive, yes, but if this was her career as youth group leader, could he stand to be with her or them for that fact? James stopped debating, flung his duffle bag, and rolled up sleeping bag on to the lower cot.

It won't be that bad.

Once the weight of the bags hit the mattress, his whole bed caved in on itself, crashing to the floor. From the top bunk, a bucket of what seemed to be dirty creek water drenched James' head to toe. Uproar of laughter and pointing fingers were aimed directly at him. James closed his eyes in frustration and swallowed the inappropriate words that ran through his head. He couldn't believe these kids were so unruly for a Christian youth group. How could they be so rude and inconsiderate? Just then, Nelson slapped James on his back with a hearty chuckle that almost made him double over.

"Man, it looks like they got you good Jimmy. But, you don't smell good."

James wasn't laughing along. And Nelson was getting on his nerves.

Where did this guy get off?

James felt like taking a swing at this guy, if it wasn't for the kids around he just might have.

Nelson turned and snickered all the way out the door. A loud cowbell could be heard from below the hill were James had parked his car. The kids went wild and disappeared as fast as they could. Wiping sludge from his face and making his way to the dark bathroom he thought.

Sleeping with the bears didn't start to sound too bad.

With a clean shirt and pair of jeans on James, he realigned the "missing" support boards from his bed back into place. He sat down on the newly sustained bed and retrieved his hiking boots. Slipping them on, he suddenly felt tired and worn out. He checked his wristwatch; it was almost ten o'clock in the morning. With despair, he fell back onto the pillow of his cot. His head hit with thump. Rolling his eyes in immediate anger, he tore the pillow from its case and pulled out the object of his injury.

It was a small, black, leather bound bible. On the front cover, a silver cross was engraved into the leather. He fanned the pages it was brand new, crisp, clean.

Ok. He thought. *Let's start over.*

Besides the two cabins for the boys and the girls respectively, there was also a lodge center building that was located between the two, for various gatherings. Attached to that building was also a dining area with tables and a small kitchen. Perfect for youth groups, convention events, or a wedding reception. Although James had never been here, he was already starting to enjoy walking around the open campus. The cowbell that everyone had heard before was the signal for everyone to convene at the lodge. James was obviously late because he had to "recompose" himself after the foul prank. He knew he would have everyone's eyes on him. So, before he entered the lodge he took some seconds to ready himself. Pushing through the front door, he entered the open room where everyone would be. Except there was no one inside, his first thought was that he was being set up for another prank at his expense. But when nothing happened, he began to be confused. Was he in the wrong place? Was this the lodge or was there another lodge they were supposed to meet in? Just before he turned to leave, a side door opened and a woman in a white apron appeared.

"Are you Jimmy?" She asked.

James didn't want to respond to that name. Correcting her, he said,

"Yes, I am James and I am looking for the youth group LIFT."

She pointed her finger toward a window.

"They told me to tell you they would be out at Baker's field."

James peered through the window and could see a large group of people off in the distance.

"Thanks." He told the woman and burst out through the same door he came in. He started with a slow jog, but gained speed and joined the group in a short time.

Eugene saw him first and met him before he reached everyone.

"Hey Jimmy, glad you made it, we actually just started."

James was a bit out of breath from the running. He shook his head, understanding Eugene.

"Find your small group of teens and get in line, we are about to start the race." With that, Eugene returned to the group. Still a bit out of breath James found his four group members and got in line behind them. Not one of them made eye contact with him. All nine of the groups were lined up across the field. Each person at the head of the line held a plastic baseball bat. Grace stepped out from her group.

"Ok, is everybody in a single line with in their group?"

A resounding yes came from the whole. She noticed James at the end of his own line and gave him a nod. He returned one back.

"Good, now, I know you are all wondering why the first person in your line is holding a bat. Well, the next thing we are going to do is a relay race."

The teens all shouted in excitement and eagerness.

"The object is to be the first team to finish. What you are going to have to do is to press the bat to your forehead and facing the ground, spin around ten times. Then run to the orange cones placed out there." Grace pointed to nine small orange cones that were spaced out a short distance away from each group. "Then return to your group and tag the next person in line and they will spin ten times and round their cone. The first team that that has all their members complete the race wins. Does everybody understand?"

Why did she even ask? Grace was answered with an enthusiastic 'yes' from all. She returned to her team and pointed to Father Warren. James hadn't seen him till now and was glad to see the man was present. He didn't expect him to be here. But James didn't have time to think about that.

"Hey, you guys." James whispered to his teammates.

"I know that you got me with you little prank and that's cool. I can take it, but right now we are a team and we have to work together if we are going to win this." He was met with some confused looking eyes. Yet, they all were shaking their heads in agreement. James placed his hand in the middle of the group.

"Slippery Mongoose on three!" Now, the others were looking at him as if his head was full of creek water. They must have liked the idea because they all put their hands in the center.

James softly counted to three and the five of them all shouted there rally call. Slippery Mongoose! They got stares of all kinds. The yell had gotten Grace's attention too and she met eyes again with James. She shot him a questioning look, all he gave her was a playful sneer.

Father Warren held up his arm.

"On your mark."

Everybody quickly reformed his or her lines.

"Get set." The priest waited a few seconds and howled. "GO!"

The race was on. James was bouncing with anticipation at the end of his line. All the adult leaders were at the end of their respective lines. James shouted in encouragement of his teammates and they ran fast. He was having a blast with this; he hadn't felt this energetic in years. Glancing around at the others, they too were getting into the event. Then he came face to face with Nelson, he pointed at James and gave him a thumbs down.

No way is he going to beat me. James thought beginning to get very competitive.

Now, it was down to the end of each line and the adult leaders were up. The race was pretty even between groups. One of the volunteer teachers group had a slight lead. Then it was Nelson's group. After that, James couldn't decide who was placed next. The dark haired boy who showed him his cot earlier came running at top speed ready to tag James's hand. With a slap, they tagged hands and James started to spin around as fast as he could as the rest of his team counted off his number of rotations. They shouted ten in unison and James took off in the direction of his orange cone. However, he was dizzier then he thought he would be. He tried to focus on his path, but his body wouldn't cooperate with his mind. It cost him some time as he regained his momentum. Ahead of him rounding his own cone, he saw Nelson who somehow seemed unaffected by the spinning. Finally, James circled his cone and sped up his pace. He was catching up to Nelson he was close. Just a little more, his legs burning, it was between the two of them. The teens all-screaming at the top of their lungs cheer them on. At the last moment, Nelson surged past James and won. Breathing hard his teammates surrounded James patting him on the back and giving words of encouragement. James couldn't believe he had lost. His heart felt like it was beating through his chest. Resting on the ground, the boy with dark hair congratulated him on a job well done. James thanked him.

Then the boy told him that it wasn't any of the teen that had pulled the prank on him. James thought he was hearing things. Confused, James asked the evident question, who? The boy pointed over to a crowd of people, and then James knew right away who had done it. He was slapping high fives and throwing his fist into the air, Nelson, couldn't help, but smile wide.

CHAPTER

20

Grace felt like she hadn't eaten all day. So, when she had finally gotten her food for lunch, she couldn't wait to dig in. After the relay race, the cowbell had rung again prompting everyone to make their way back to the lodge for lunch. Lunch was served in the dinning room. The room was dotted throughout with large round tables able to sit six people around each. Long white table clothes draped over a head table in the front of the room. The youth group adults all sat at it. The room was clearly laid out for a wedding reception. A buffet table was along a far wall, it covered more than enough food for the group. One of the best things about Lake Forest was that the staff served three meals for the weekend, lunch and dinner on Saturday, then on Sunday morning a light breakfast. The meals were excellent the only problem was that it made the retreat expensive for LIFT. So, that is why they usually made the trip for autumn instead of the busy summer months. The weather was a bit colder, but they were given a discounted price.

Grace looked around the dinning room as she sat down at a place amongst the adults at the head table.

Most of all the teens were crowded around the circular tables and eating. The only person Grace didn't seem to see was James. Where was he? They all had been in the dinning room for almost twenty minutes already. Maybe he wasn't hungry. Grace caught Kathy's attention as she sat down in a chair on Grace's right.

"Hey, have you seen James around?" Grace asked her.

"Who? Oh Jimmy. Umm..." Kathy took a glace around the room.

"No, not since out in the field." She looked round the room once more, and then gave Grace an innocent expression.

"Oh, by the way Grace." Kathy said changing the topic and turning fully in her seat in the direction of Grace. "I wanted to go over some things that I added to my talk."

Grace leaned in giving Kathy her full attention as she took a few bites of her potatoes. Kathy started talking, reviewing her new changes with Grace. No one must have noticed James enter, they where all too busy eating or talking to one another. He strode to the head table. Grace too must have not been paying attention; she was lost in conversation with Kathy. The black leather bible slammed down hard on the table top right in front of Grace. She jumped at the sound. James stood motionless in front of her staring. Nelson piped up saying.

"Hey, Jimmy, what's up?"
James didn't even turn his head, he stayed focused on Grace. She was frozen at his display.

"I don't need this." James finally said indicating the bible. "I am packing my things and leaving."

He then faced everyone else at the head table and announced to them.

"And my name is NOT Jimmy! It's James!" With that, he bolted from the room. The whole head table put their gaze on Grace. She was shocked she didn't know what to do. Should she go after him?

James pushed open the front doors of the lodge in anger. As he started up the path to the boy's cabin, he heard her voice call from behind him.

"James." It hollered. "James, wait."

He kept moving toward his destination.

"James, please." It begged.

He stopped and turned facing Grace as she caught up to him, her blonde ponytail bouncing with each step.

"You know this is all because of you." He said sharply, pointing a finger at her. "If you never would have hit my car, I wouldn't be here." Again, she was speechless, but this time, the words hurt. She handed him the bible back.

"This was a gift from me." Grace took a deep breath. "And you can leave if you would like, but I want you to stay." Emotion poured out from her words. She felt something for him, a longing, and a connection, something that couldn't be explained. She continued talking. "I'm not the only one who wants you here either. I have heard and been told by quite a few teens you're a pretty cool guy and lots of fun." She looked at James tenderly. "I can see it in you. The way you interact with your group or the way you were eager to get here today."

James gripped the bible in his hands. He felt proud, he didn't know the teens thought this way about him or Grace did for that matter.

"You do what you want, but before you do, take a listen to your heart...what does it say?"

James was clearly thinking for a moment. Grace held up her hands in front of him.

"Don't decide now. Take some time." Try and pray about it, see what God wants you to do."

James had never done that before, but took Grace's advice to mind.

"I heard about the prank this morning. It was rude and uncalled for. From now on I'll handle Nelson." Grace certainly knew how to take charge of a situation.

James was still impressed though that he himself had made such an impression on her and the teens.

"I gave you the bible, because, I believe you have a lot of questions and in it you can find your answers."

He looked down at the book. He suddenly felt horrible for yelling at her. She didn't deserve that kind of behavior. She was only trying to help him. He wanted to tell her, but she turned back toward the lodge and went inside. Alone, James continued up the trail into the woods.

Back inside the dinning room, Grace, retook her place at the head table. Her food, now cold, almost uneaten, sat in front of her. She lost her appetite; all she could think about was James. She truly hoped he would stay, although she didn't want to push him into anything he didn't want.

Grace knew everyone at the table wanted to know what had happened, but she would leave them in suspense. She also knew Nelson's motives behind the dirty prank. Wiping her thoughts clear reminded herself that this weekend wasn't about personal problems, it was for the teens. Returning her mindset to the weekend; she couldn't help but think the decision James would make would be beyond her. God was in control and He would guide him. The dinning room door opened as James came through it. He made his way to the buffet table. Picking up a plate started loading it with food. Grace was bursting inside with joy; she could hardly hold back her radiant smile. God was good.

Instead of taking a place with the other adults at the head table, James found a spot among a group of teens. They scooted themselves making room for him. Again, James had overcome Grace's previous judgments about him.

With their bellies full and energy levels back to normal, the teens were all ready for the next activity for the weekend. Everybody had broken up into their small groups. They waited patiently in the large open convention room, as Grace started to reveal what was next. Kathy walked to the front of the room and stood aside of Grace. She introduced Kathy to everyone and then turned the audience over to her. Grace took a seat on the floor within her own small group. James thought Kathy looked nervous up there in front, as she started her talk. The topic was on God's gifts. Kathy read a bible verse and James quickly opened his bible, hunting for it. It was no use; he had no idea of how to find it. James had never read the bible before, he was unfamiliar with it. He had heard bible verse before in Sunday school when he was young and here and there through out life, but had never owned a bible or much less ever read one in his spare time. Until Grace prompted him to try it just a half-hour ago, when she had left him to decide whether to stay or leave Lake Forest. Journeying into the woods and sitting on the moist ground, he searched his thoughts and for the first time in a long time, he slowed down. His mind had been in a panic lately with him losing his job. Having a good career was all he ever strived for. James decided to take Grace's counsel. He opened his heart, asking God for an answer, he was met with nothing. Why wouldn't it work? He needed to know what to do. He suddenly felt silly and stupid, sitting in the woods waiting for an answer from some almighty being. He stood to leave in hopes to never run into Grace again. Something stirred in the nature around him. The trees swayed as if being moved in a direction not their own. Was there something bigger out of life? A brisk wind hit James for just a moment and he realized that he had stopped worrying about his current unemployment. The release of pressure was amazing. Instead, he thought about what he was ultimately motivated to do in his life. Another idea that Grace had given him popped into his head. If this didn't work he would leave. Part of him wished it would. Picking up the leather bound bible, James fanned the pages. What made him do this, he wasn't sure, but he wanted an answer now, he couldn't wait. He stopped fanning and just opened the book to a page. With his finger, he pointed to a spot in the text. The section of the text, he had found read this.

Be still before the Lord and wait patiently for Him; do not fret when men succeed in their ways, when they carry out their wicked schemes.

That was all James needed to read.

Now, as Kathy was closing with her talk, all James could think about was how he longed to know more. Something was building inside him again, a feeling of clarity, hope, and newness.

Eugene came around to each group, handing each group leader a white piece of paper. When James received his, he read what was printed on it. A list of two questions, they were discussion questions for each small group to talk about. The questions came from Kathy's talk she had just given. James realized he hadn't even been listening to Kathy. He had been lost in his own thoughts. The four teens in his group all looked blankly at him. He had to say something. He read the first question to them.

1.   As in the reading Romans 12:6-8. What do you see as your God Gift?

James thought quickly and handed his bible over to one of the girls in the group, she was covered in freckles. He asked her to find and re-read the passage. With lightning speed, she located the book, chapter, and verse. James was stunned at her capability.

"We have different gifts, according to the grace given us. If a man's gift is prophesying, let him use it in proportion to his faith. If it is serving, let him serve; if it is teaching, let him teach; if it is encouraging, let him encourage; if it is contributing to the needs of others, let him give generously; if it is leadership, let him govern diligently; if it is showing mercy, let him do it cheerfully."

The girl returned the bible to James who kept it open to the page it was on. He read the question again to them. For a moment, he contemplated his own answer. What was his gift from God? The dark haired boy in the group spoke up saying.

"I think my God gift is honesty." The boy sounded so sure of himself as if he knew that the 'honesty' was his answer even before the question was read. The girl sitting next to him, the one who had read the verse spoke next.

"Mine, I guess, would be compassion."
Chiming in after her the second girl in the group said.

"Yeah, I believe that is mine too, compassion."

They shared an innocence look and smiled at each other. All eyes fell on the last boy sitting in the small circle. He looked as though he was thinking hard about his answer. Finally, he spoke up with a grin on his face.

"My God gift is probably patience."
James was impressed with each teen's answer to the question. Yet, he was still at a loss for his own God gift. He moved on to the second question, reading it aloud.

"How do you use this God gift in your life?"

Again, one by one, each teen answered the question. As they went around the circle, James tried to comprehend how they all seemed to be able to apply God to their own life. They knew how He worked in them. How had He worked in James life? He didn't seem to be able to think of any situation or event in his own life. Nothing stood out in his mind, was God really in his life?

"James, what is your gift?" the girl with the freckles asked. James was in mid-thought, he felt blank; what was going he going to tell them? That he was second guessing himself? That God wasn't in his life or that he had no relationship with Him whatsoever? James had to say something. Didn't that bible verse he read in the woods connect to him? Or was it something he just wanted to hear? The teens waited for his answer.

"Ok, everyone." Grace announced. "Let's head back outside to Baker's Field."

Everybody rose from their small groups and started for the door. James bent the corner of the page in the bible they had been on, marking it for later. Just when he thought he might understand God, he was back where he had started, confusion and doubt. How was he supposed to connect to Him? James' brain was clouded with more questions now than ever.

21

Being outside again was exhilarating, the fresh, cool air, combined with the warming sun. James breathed in his surroundings as the youth group made their way to the open field. He thought over the two questions about God's gifts on the way over. He needed more understanding on the subject, which made him wish he had paid better attention to Kathy's talk. He could approach her and ask about the talk; then again, James didn't feel like he knew her well enough to be asking questions about a topic she had just finished explaining about. He didn't want to embarrass himself with her, although he had made quite the display by storming into the dinning room and lashing out at the adults at the head table.

The only person James felt he could truly talk to is Grace. But he didn't see her. She must have gotten ahead of him in the group. James searched her out amid the crowd. There, toward the front of the mob, she was walking with two other young girls. He walked up to her; being closer, he noticed her tossing a red rubber ball from hand to hand. With a quick movement, James snatched the ball from Grace's possession. She was caught off her guard by James' speed. Walking backward facing Grace and the girls, he now held the red ball pretending it was his hostage.

"Hey!" Grace exclaimed. James smiled at her.

"Can we talk?" He asked with a serious tone in his voice.

Nodding her head Grace answered. "Sure."

James tossed over the ball to the girls, who giggled to each other quietly.

James and Grace pulled off the main path. They let the rest of the group pass by and entered the field.

Unsure of what he really wanted to say to Grace or how to phrase it, he was glad she spoke first.

"I'm really glad you stayed, I understand your reasons for wanting to leave. I'm sure it was a difficult decision for you to make." James was starting to feel uncomfortable for some reason. Grace was so easy to talk to, why couldn't he just tell her what he was feeling?

"So, what did you want to talk about?"

Grace was so beautiful, sweet, and patient with him. The wind blew a few strands of her blonde hair in her face. Her delicate hand pushed them behind her ear. He inhaled deeply and just said it.

"Can you tell me what my God gift is?" Grace saw it again in his expression this time, a movement awakening inside him.

"I wish I could, but you and God are the only ones who know that." She replied. It was a bit of a letdown for James, but in the same sense, he was fascinated by the mystery of God and how He worked.

"Grace, I want to have what you have." She didn't seem to be really sure what James was trying to say. He went on.

"You seem happy, fulfilled in a way that I don't."

Now she knew what he was getting at. Swaying back and forth, talking with his hands, James was nervous. Grace thought it was cute.

"It's because I have a relationship with Jesus Christ."

Shaking his head in understanding, James was beginning to see the idea. He knew who Jesus was, heck who didn't. But to have a relationship with him was little more than he was looking for.

"Jesus said in John 14:6, I am the way and the truth and the life. No one come through the Father except through me."

James thought that was quite a bold statement for one man to give. Grace could see, James still looked confused. From the field, Eugene called over to them.

"Hey, listen is it ok if we talk later some more about this?" She asked James.

"That's fine with me." He said still thinking over Jesus' claim. Grace started walking to join the group in the field; she turned back to James mid way.

"It'll be a date." She said raising her eyebrows.
WOW. James couldn't believe Grace had just said that. Why did she say that? Was she just joking around? Her expression on her face didn't say she was. He didn't care he couldn't keep the smile off his own face. Grace was certainly a unique girl and James found himself falling for her.

Despite the cooler weather, everyone seemed to be sweating in some respect. The youth group had gathered in Baker's Field for an annual LIFT weekend retreat kickball game. Nevertheless, this wasn't just any kind of kickball game it was girls versus boys. A match up that was very evenly paired. There seemed to be equally number of boys and girls, so each side wasn't out numbered by the other. As far as the game itself went, the score was close as well.

The boys were up by one point making the score 12-11. The girls were up to kick and there were two outs. It being the final winning of the game, this was the girl's last effort to regain the lead. With two girls on base, first and second, respectfully the boys only had to make one more out to end the game and claim the winning title.

Grace was inching her way off second and ready to make a scoring run home as the girl's next kicker came to the plate. James, out of breath and more tired then he had felt in long time, was keeping a close eye on the runners. He stood ready for the next play at shortstop. Nelson was pitching the ball and Eugene catching. The rest of the teen boys were scattered through out the field also ready to make the final out. Up walked the girl with freckles, the one in James' small group. She looked like she could kick the ball into the next county. James gave her a playful holler egging her on how she kicked like a girl and so forth. Grace yelled back at him.

"She is a girl and she going to win this game for us." Grace was determined to win. This was one of here favorite games during the weekend nothing would stop her. She was also thrilled that James really did end up staying. She had prayed he would. Lately, he was all she could think about. His curiosity about her faith and his interaction with LIFT made him different from the other guys that Grace had known. Now, as she watched the girl boot the red rubber ball high into the air she shot from her base and ran as fast as she could. The ball was kicked hard off to James' left out deep into the field. Coming right toward him Grace was running full speed, he watched as the boys in the outfield threw the ball toward home base to get her out. They weren't going to beat her in time and Grace knew it too. As she ran past James, he clutched his arms around her waist trying to hold her in place. She screamed and squealed lightheartedly. The whole field went wild shouting and roaring, the boys howling for James to hold tight and the girls yelping for her release. James was stronger than Grace had thought. She wiggled and squirmed digging her feet into the dirt trying to break free.

Laughing at how much fun she was having, Grace thought of an idea. Twisting her body and coming face to face with James, she wrapped her arms around his neck, looked him straight in the eyes, and kissed him on the lips. Instantly she was free off and running. James surpassed by the kiss and knocked off his momentum tripped backward landing him on his back flat on the ground.

The crowd went into frenzy as Grace and the other two girls made it to home base in time to score. All the girls gathered around home base chanting their victory. Cheering and celebrating they laughed and giggled at their opponents, especially James, who was still lying on the ground. He was amazed at what had just happened. Staring up at the blue sky above he felt a powerful sensation come over him. He was in love.

After the exhausting, but unbelievable game of kickball, it was nice to be able to sit down for a while. Everyone had gathered again in the open convention room, divided into their individual small groups. It was time for another talk from an adult leader. This time Eugene stood up in the front readying himself for his speech. He shuffled papers and took a sip of water before he began. This time James was intent on paying attention; he didn't want to miss a single word. Yet, after the events during the kickball how could he possibly focus. James leaned back his arms propping him up as he lay on the floor. He kept watching Grace from the corner of his eye. Every few minutes she would look over at him with a look of candidness. James couldn't even believe what was happening. Love, true love, or so he thought. He had never felt this before. He had dated a couple of times in high school and college, but those girls didn't have what Grace did. He was consumed with thoughts for her.

Eugene cleared his throat and started talking. His topic was on forgiveness. James listened closely as Eugene gave examples of how Jesus forgave tax collectors, murderers, thieves, even prostitutes. What was this forgiveness that they wanted and why did they want it from a man sent from God? Who was Jesus truly? A man who came just to die? It was all pretty vague to James. He would have to ask Grace when they talked again. Wait a minute. Would it be different now between him and Grace? Was she just teasing James? How did she really feel about him? Something was going on. He wanted to talk to Grace about that too.

Eugene now talked about forgiveness toward one another, how we should be forgiving people and not egotistical or boastful with others. Some of the things Eugene was saying were hitting home with James. He thought back to the car accident and how he acted toward Grace. Further back James thought about Thomas and their past differences. How it all could have been avoided and handled differently. James started to feel remorseful. He made the promise to himself that when he returned home, James would tell Thomas everything. He would explain to him about losing his job, how he struggled getting a job, and why he had never taken a position within Thomas' company. James started to feel proud. He felt good about confronting Thomas. God and Jesus, well actually faith in general was never really a topic or an issue when James was growing up and living with Thomas. He wondered what kind of faith life Thomas had now that he was getting married to Jan.

Eugene finished his talk with a prayer to Jesus asking Him to have forgiveness on all of us and for us to share forgiveness with each other. This time Martha passed around white pieces of paper with questions on them. The small group discussions went much better in James' group and he was learning a lot about each of the teens in his group. James was really starting to enjoy LIFT. He liked having the teens look up to him. Even though he might not know how to answer every question they had, but this was something he considered he would like to be more involved in.

22

After the small group discussions were finished, everybody took a half hour break in the dinning room to refuel. James was sitting at a table full of boys who were all giving him a hard time about getting tricked by Grace's kissing maneuver. All James could do was to shake his head in defense; he didn't know what to say to them.

"Sorry guys, she caught me off guard." James tried to explain.

"Yeah, she caught you off guard alright; she just about knocked you right out of you boots." The boy with dark hair that was in his small group said. James remembered his God gift as being honest and the kid sure was being honest. He laughed right along with the rest of them. Then the boys started to get quiet and eyeing someone behind James, one boy spoke saying.

"Here she comes right now."

Grace walked up to the table and leaned on the edge acting like she is one of them.

"Hey, boys mind if I talk to James for a minute?"

They of course all hooted and howled making kissing noises and all darted in different directions leaving the two alone.

Grace sat down in a chair next to James.

"So, what do you call that tactic you used?" Grace gave an innocent smile.

"Oh ha ha, like I'm going to tell you." She pushed a half piece of paper over to him.

"What's this, a love note?" He asked.

"No, it's for our next activity." James took the paper and read it.

PONTIUS PILATE –

Pilate: "I find no basis for a charge against this man. You brought me this man as one who was inciting the people to rebellion. I have examined him in your presence and have found no basis for your charges against him. Neither has Herod, for he sent him back to us; as you can see, he has done nothing to deserve death."

James looked up at Grace.

"We need someone to play Pontius Pilate. Do you think you could do it? All you have to do is read the lines of the dialogue."

James wasn't really sure what this was for, but he agreed anyway because he wanted to be helpful to the group.

"Great, Eugene will tell you where to stand and give you your costume."

Costume, what costume? James thought. What had he agreed to?

As she rose from her seat, she gave him one of her sweet smiles and continued on her way. James re-read the paper in his hands. Who was Pontius Pilate?

The sun was starting to set and the weather was cooling down as evening approached. James and Eugene walked together out past Baker's Field and out even further than that.

"So, what's this all about, what are we doing?" James asked.

"We are going to reenact the crucifixion of Jesus."

Both men were dressed in heavy white cloths over their own clothes. The white garments were draped over their right shoulders, across their bodies and tied together around the waist with a piece of gold rope. The costumes were both very similar, but James wore a red cape with his that flowed behind him. Eugene stopped walking and looked around to make sure he was in the right place.

"Ok, this is the spot; just stay here until the group comes by. You will be prompted by Father Warren to read your part. He is going to play the narrator. Do you have your lines?"

James held up the half sheet of paper indicating he did.

"Good. Then when we are done at this station, just follow behind the group, but stay in character to keep it realistic."

James understood what he had to do. Eugene gave him a thumbs-up and told him he was going to be great. Before he turned to leave, James spoke asking,

"Eugene, who was Pontius Pilate in the story? What was his connection to the crucifixion?"

Eugene edged up closer to James and looked intently serious.

"He is the one who sentenced Jesus to the crucifixion."

The realization hit James hard. Eugene left James and walked down out of the woods back across the field in the direction of the lodge.

Again, James was alone in the woods. His thoughts swarmed around the idea of Jesus and what he really did to deserve death at the hands of the people He was trying to save.

James wandered around a bit thinking back to what Grace had said about her relationship with Jesus. What had she quoted from what Jesus said? All those who want to get to the Father must go through Him. How was he supposed to do that? He didn't feel Jesus calling out to him, inviting James into a relationship with Him. James wished he had his bible with him. More so, he wished that Grace were there with him to answer his questions. What was happening between them? Was it something more than just a friendship and what about that kiss? James gazed out across the field and saw the group coming in his direction.

A couple of teens held fiery torches that lit up the growing darkness of the impending night that was to come. Leading the group were Nelson and Eugene. Nelson was walking slowly draped in a red cloth similar to what James was wearing. A crown of sharp looking thorns, which was made out of toothpicks, sat on his head. The look on Nelson's face was melancholy with a hint of acceptance.

He played the part of Jesus well. Then James spotted Grace. Her blonde hair had been curled and layered and she was covered in a long light blue fabric. She strode solemnly along with the group; James wasn't sure what part she was portraying. She looked magnificent though.

James stood ready to deliver his dialogue to them.

A small silence came over the group as winds tried to blow out the torches. Nelson walked up and stood next to James facing the others hanging his head. Father Warren, who was standing off to the side read his part of the narrator.

"Then Pilate announced to the chief priests and the crowd saying."

James read his lines with as much believability as he could.

"I find no basis for a charge against this man. You brought me this man as one who was inciting the people to rebellion. I have examined him in your presence and have found no basis for your charges against him. Neither has Herod, for he sent him back to us; as you can see, he has done nothing to deserve death."

Then Father Warren read some more.

"But with loud shouts the crowd insistently demanded that he be crucified, and their shouts prevailed. So Pilate decided to grant their demand. He released the man who had been thrown into prison for insurrection and murder, the one they asked for, and surrendered Jesus to their will." (Luke 23: 1-25)

James some how felt sick to himself. As if he really had sentenced Jesus to his death. The moment was unnerving.

The group moved on to the next station and James followed staying toward the back, where he found Father Warren. He walked along the outside of the group, hands clasped behind his back holding his narrator's script. The man looked reverent as he stepped through the woods. Everyone stopped and Nelson kneeled down in the cold grass, head slumped downward. Then Father Warren explained the scene that was happening before them.

"Then the soldiers of the governor took Jesus into the governor's headquarters, and then gathered the whole cohort around him. They stripped him and put a scarlet robe on him, and after twisting some thorns into a crown, they put it on his head. They put a reed in his right hand and knelt before him and mocked him, saying, 'Hail, King of the Jews!' They spat on him, and took the reed and struck him on the head. After mocking him, they stripped him of the robe and put his own clothes on him. Then they led him away to crucify him." (Matthew 27.27-31)

A cross, constructed from the two by four which James had purchased, was set upon Nelson's shoulder. Eugene, playing the solider, laughed at him and kicked at him to be on his way. The cross probably didn't weigh very much, but Nelson did a good job of making everyone believe it did. He pushed upward struggling to stand, finally he stood erect. Then slowly he began walking, the cross' long beam dragging in the grass and dirt behind him.

The teens seemed stunned at Nelson's display, as if it was truly the Man, Jesus before them. It took them a minute to follow him to the next station. They hadn't been walking very long when all of a sudden, Nelson went sprawling down to the ground with the cross. Quickly, Father Warren stepped in and said,

"Surely he took up our infirmities and carried our sorrows, yet we considered him stricken by God, smitten by Him, and afflicted. But he was pierced for our transgressions, he was crushed for our iniquities; the punishment that brought us peace was upon him, and by his wounds we are healed. We all, like sheep, have gone astray, each of us has turned to his own way; and the Lord has laid on him the iniquity of us all." (Isaiah 53:4-6)

Breaking away from the crowd, Martha dressed in dark blue and white approached Nelson as he returned to his feet. She took her hands and placed them on his face. Father Warren again spoke up describing her emotions.

"Now as it all took place. In her heart she had kept the words of the angel, spoken to her in the beginning: "Do not be afraid, Mary."" (Luke 1:30).

Nelson moved on step by step wavering as if he was ready to fall again. Eugene looked into the crowd and grabbed one of the taller boys by his shirt. The boy's eyes went wide and he protested as Eugene picked up the end of the cross and handed it to him. Totally caught out of surprise of what was happening, the tall boy took the wooden cross in his own arms and helped Nelson carry the weight. The group continued to move along. As they marched, Father Warren narrated.

"As they led him away, they seized Simon from Cyrene, who was on his way in from the country, and put the cross on him and made him carry it behind Jesus." (Luke 23:26)

They whole group was now about half way across Baker's Field. Nelson and the tall boy slugged on, walking in silence. Beautiful Grace, now made her way toward the front of the line, James watched as she removed a cloth from her pocket. Wiping Nelson's face with it, she stood aside in obvious sorrow.

"My heart says of you 'Seek his face!' Your face, Lord, I will seek. Do not hide your face from me, do not turn your servant away in anger; you have been my helper.

Do not reject me or forsake me, O God my Savior."

Father Warren read as they moved on past Grace. She caught up again to the group in the back close to James. He was very much entranced in the proceedings to even notice her by him. James was more intent on what was going to happen next. Then it happened; Nelson fell to the hard, cold, ground again. The tall boy gripped the cross in his arms, but couldn't hold on to it. It came crashing down next to Nelson. Eugene pulled on Nelson's arm and back onto his wobbling feet. The cross was laid back on his shoulder as Nelson stood a moment as the crowd looked on awestruck. Again, Father Warren read explaining.

"He was despised and rejected by men, a man of sorrows, and familiar with suffering. Like one from whom men hide their faces he was despised, and we esteemed him not." (Isaiah 53:3).

Then Father read more saying.

"A large number of people followed him, including women who mourned and wailed for him. Jesus turned and said to them, "Daughters of Jerusalem, do not weep for me; weep for yourselves and for your children." (Luke 23:27-28)

The three volunteer women clothed all in brown and white cloths, Cried uncontrollably at the sight before them. At first, James thought they were faking it pretty good. But as he drew closer, tears were truly on their faces. Moved by the events, which were happening before them. James was impressed by them because they didn't hold back their emotions. As he turned his attention back to rest of the group, Nelson crumpled to the ground hard for the third time. Yelling at him to get up, the solider, Eugene kicked him a few times. He shouted more at Nelson that he couldn't die so easily here in the road. Picking himself up with incredible strength, Nelson took up the cross once again and moved on. Then the voice of Father Warren read.

> "Do not withhold your mercy from me, O Lord; may your love and your truth always protect me. For troubles without number surround me; my sins have overtaken me, and I cannot see. They are more than the hairs of my head, and my heart fails within me. Be pleased, O Lord, to save me; O Lord, come quickly to help me." (Psalm 40:11-13)

Everyone walked a little while longer through the field. Eugene stopped Nelson and took the cross from him. Nelson looked ready to collapse with exhaustion. With his hands, Eugene ripped down the red cloth that Nelson wore exposing his chest. Standing the cross in a support slot in the ground, Nelson was backed into it. Eugene stretched out Nelson's arms across the middle beam of the cross. Imitating swinging a hammer slammed down on both of Nelson's hands and feet. He screamed in agony as the invisible nails pierced his body. As this happened, Father Warren read aloud.

"So the soldiers took charge of Jesus. Carrying his own cross, he went out to the place of the Skull. Here they crucified him, and with him two others—one on each side and Jesus in the middle."

A couple of teens in the group had tears in their eyes. Others held hands with the person next to them. James had never seen such a presentation of such emotion and passion.

Father Warren continued to speak.

"From noon on, darkness came over the whole land until three in the afternoon. And about three o'clock Jesus cried with a loud voice, 'Eli, Eli, lema sabachthani?' that is, 'My God, my God, why have you forsaken me?' Then Jesus cried again with a loud voice and breathed his last. Now when the centurion and those with him, who were keeping watch over Jesus, saw what took place, they were terrified and said, 'Truly this man was God's Son!'" (Matthew 27.45-46,50,54)

"Soon, then Jesus was taken down from the cross and laid in an empty tomb. His body was wrapped in a linen cloth and spices and oils were used at the burial."

Eugene and the tall boy took Nelson into their arms and carried him away.

Silence gripped the moment filling the night air, as the last bits of daylight crept away giving into night. Grace walked to the front of the group and told everyone to sit. It felt good to James to sit down; the day's events were starting to wear on him. Grace took a moment and looked through the group, and then she pointed back at the cross that stood behind her.

"He died for you." She waited a minute to let it sink in. "He died for your sins, the sins of your past, present and future. So that we all could have eternal life with Him in heaven."

Grace had everyone's complete attention. "What you saw here tonight was not just the death of a man. It was a resurrection of life. Because three days later, Jesus rose from his grave showing us He conquered death too."

Some of the teens smiled as they listened. "All He wants in return from us is our love and praise in a relationship with Him." Grace took a relaxing breath. "But, this relationship with Jesus can't be forced or negotiated. It has to be of your own will. He knows your pains, worries, doubts, and fears. He is here to comfort them. He is waiting for you, longing to be with you. All you have to do is ask Him into your heart."
Grace took another glace around at the ready faces.

"You've seen how He suffered for you; take a moment tonight to give something back to Him. Ask Him to be part of your life, pray with Him, I guarantee you won't regret it."

Grace simply said everything James was yearning to hear. The crucifixion reenactment was stunning to him, but Grace's words cemented his every disbelief. This is what he wanted, what he was missing from his life, a relationship with Jesus in his heart. James felt soulfully complete.

23

The head table in the dinning room was empty as everyone gathered for dinner. Instead of sitting at it, all the adults were seated amongst the teens, a prompt taken from James to get to know them better. Dinner tasted good considering they were all physically tired from the kickball game as well as emotionally worn out from the moving crucifixion reenactment followed by Grace's uplifting talk. James carried his plate over to the table where Nelson was sitting, placing himself in a seat next to him. He took a couple of bites from his burger washing it down with a gulp of water. James turned to Nelson.

"I thought you did an excellent job portraying Jesus. It was stunningly believable."

Nelson nodded his head replying. "Thanks."

They each ate some of their food. James was truthful in what he had said. Nelson's representation of Jesus was quite remarkable.

"So, did you play Jesus last year too?" James asked.

Nelson finished chewing the bite he had just taken. Shaking his head in response as he swallowed.

"No, this is my first time on this trip." James was shocked; he had thought that Nelson had done this many times before.

"Actually, I just recently became an adult leader with LIFT."

James was under the impression that he was the only new person to join. It was a bit of a relief to hear this news.

"I've been meaning to tell you sorry, James."
It was odd to hear Nelson call him James instead of Jimmy.

"Oh yeah?" James said with a hint of sarcasm. Nelson arched an eyebrow at him continuing.

"About the creek water prank, by now I'm sure you know it was me." He took his eyes off James and stared in the distance. Nelson visibly wasn't the apologizing type.

"And I am sorry for calling you "Jimmy"." James nodded in acceptance. Combing his hair back with his fingers, Nelson sighed openly.

"I did all that because I didn't want to be the new guy, not knowing what was going to on. I'm not really so good with kids, especially teens."

James calmly listened to Nelson who was clearly uncomfortable with explaining himself.

"I didn't know why I even came out here, just sort of happened."

James could easily relate to him. It was as if he was partly talking to himself in some respect.

"Then I found out you were coming, then the whole retreat turning into a competition for me."

James was bewildered, a competition? How did he see a youth group retreat weekend as a competition?

"Oh, because of the small group activities and kickball game?" James asked. Nelson shook his head slowly returning his gaze back at James.

"Because of Grace."

James didn't understand, why Grace? What did this weekend have to do with her?

"At first, I was just messing around with you, then I told everybody you liked to be called "Jimmy"."

Nelson looked away again. James was still having trouble figuring out how this all involved Grace.

"Then when we got here before you, I told the teens if they wanted see something hilarious. That was when I setup the broken door and the bucket of water."

James figured as much, yet how did the pranks have to do with Grace?

"So, how does Grace fit into all of it?" James finally said.

"Well, the Sunday night you came to return Grace's driver license, she told us, the adults, you were the guy who humiliated her the day of the car accident."

It was all coming together now in James's head.

"So, everybody was treating me differently because of how I had rudely acted toward Grace?"

Nelson nodded again.

"Yeah, that is everybody, but Grace. When she told us that she had invited you to this weekend, we all tried to talk her out of it. Yet, she was adamant about you coming along. She said she saw something in you, that God was working inside of you."

James was blown away by his statement, he didn't know Grace had fought for him in this way.

"She is pretty great, isn't she?"

James agreed with Nelson.

The two men sat in silence a while. James let the conversation they had just had settle in. Grace really was amazing, always looking out for others well-being instead of her own. Then something that Nelson had said didn't make sense.

"What did you mean when you said the weekend turned into a competition?"

Nelson perked up in his seat.

"Well, awhile back, before I joined LIFT. Grace and I dated a couple of times. Martha and Kathy set us up together. I thought Grace was a fantastic girl, she thought otherwise of me. But, I'll let her fill you in on the details." Nelson took a drink of water. "And I guess I've always had the idea about another chance with her."

He pointed at James.

"So, you came into the picture and Grace couldn't stop talking about you, I knew right then that I had to knock you out of the game."

Nelson laughed a little, presumably at himself.

"Clearly that didn't work and Grace has made her choice."

Was he her choice? James thought, but he was too embarrassed to ask Nelson.

"Hey, no hard feelings?"

Nelson stretched out his hand and put on a small smirk. James gripped the man's hand. A tall boy, the one who had played Simon in the crucifixion reenactment, came walking up to them. His arms were full of what looked like stereo equipment.

"Nelson, I'm going to need your help setting this up."

Acknowledging the boy, Nelson took a handful of the equipment. He gave one last nod of assurance to James and then he and the tall boy were off.

"Hey, is there anything I can do to help?"

James called after them.

Nelson turned his head around in mid-step answering.

"Nope, just go find Grace."

With that, they were out of the dinning room. James now stood and cleared his trash from his table. Wiping his hands on a napkin, he knew what he had to do. Just as Nelson had said, he had to find Grace.

"Ow!" Nelson shouted as Grace adjusted the toothpick crown of thorns atop his head.

"Well, be glad I don't push them in further." She snapped back at him. Nelson adjusted his red cloth that came across his body.

"Hold still dear." Martha instructed as she was trying to keep from burning Grace's head with the curling iron in her hair. Kathy slipped on her own white cloth and tightened the rope belt around her waist. The four of them were putting finishing touches on each others costumes for the crucifixion reenactment. Eugene pushed through the back kitchen door and checked his own fabric from behind him.

"I think this tore on my way back here." He held part of his red cape that was now almost in two pieces. Kathy scooped up some scissors attending to Eugene's cape. Martha set the curling iron down and stood back, taking a looking at Grace.

"There Grace you're all finished." Grace looked over at Eugene.

"Do you think he'll be ok up there by himself?"

He said implying James, who Eugene had just stationed out in the woods. Eugene nodded in favor as Kathy cut and adjusted his cape.

"We should just leave him up there, let him think for a while." Nelson said under his breath, but loud enough for everyone to hear. Grace threw her arms in the air and sighed loudly.

"That's enough! I know it was you with that dirty prank you pulled on him and how you've all been calling him "Jimmy". That's it! Is this the way Christians are supposed to behave?" She said aiming her words at everyone in the kitchen.

"We are here to set an example for those teens out there. Not fuel them with misjudgments of what LIFT stands for." The others stood motionless listening to Grace and feeling remorseful. But Nelson wasn't through with his own thoughts.

"Come on Grace, this guy deserves to get some pranks pulled on him. Matter of fact, I'm surprised he is still here."
Grace quickly turned and faced Nelson with anger in her words.

"He is still here because he wants to be. He wants to know more. He is willing to learn about faith and God and I wouldn't take that away from anyone." She thought that would shut Nelson up. It didn't.

"It sounds like God's not the only reason he's sticking around. We all saw you kiss him on the kickball field. Apparently there is something else going on here as well." He crossed his arms in confidence. Grace stood quiet for a moment and touched her silver cross that hung around her neck. She slowed her thoughts down rethinking the situation.

"Honestly, yes, there is something going on. But, I truly don't know myself. James was put in my life for a reason and until I figure that out, I am going to continue praying to God to lead me in the right direction."
She looked around the room tenderly.

"I need friends and support right now and you guys are all I've got."

"We're sorry, Grace." Kathy gave her a hug.

"Don't tell me, tell James." She said eyeing Nelson. The kitchen door that led to the dinning room opened and Father Warren poked his head in.

"We are all ready out here."

They all made their way to the door. Grace stopped Nelson before he went through, putting her hand on his shoulder. He looked at her.

"I made you Jesus for a reason. I knew you could bring the passion and heart out in the role." She straightened out his red sash and centered his pointed crown.

"But, don't do it for me, do it for the ones who might not know what Jesus did for us all."

Nelson gave a half smile understanding her and reached up squeezing Grace's hand.

"I will."

Then they joined the others in the dinning room.

The convention room, where they had had most of the talks that day, looked as though it has been converted into a dance club. The room was mostly dark, save for some Christmas lights that were strung overhead as if they were stars in the sky. A few teens and Nelson huddled in the corner of the room connecting wires and preparing speakers. Other teens ran around lining up chairs along the wall to clear space. James wasn't sure of what was going on. Eugene entered the room just as a colored globe lit up shooting colors of light out, illuminating the walls with spots of multicolor dots. A few kids clapped at the bright orb as it spun shinning around, moving the colors through out the room. James used the lights to find his way over to Eugene. He saw James coming over.

"Hey James."

"What's going on?" James asked him.

"Well, this year we thought we would host a little dance. Letting the teens kind of party and relax. Giving us adults some time to take a breath too."

"It certainly has been an exhausting day for everyone." Eugene agreed with him. A bunch of squealing came from the speakers giving out a whine of feedback. It quickly stopped and a couple of teens laughed in the direction of the noise. Then came Nelson's voice from a microphone.

"Sorry." He stood behind the stereo equipment with a flashlight shining up his workspace.

"Ok, all you groovers out there, are you ready for some tunes?"

He was answered with a resounding "Yeah!". The speakers crackled a bit as the teens gathered in the empty space they had made for dancing. Jolting polka music came blaring out of the speakers. The teens all howled and protested. Nelson raised his arms in confusion, as if he couldn't hear them. James and Eugene burst out with laughter each giving Nelson a thumbs-up. The teens continued to shout in detest as a few actually started dancing to the music. The polka music cut out and a mixed dance club song belted out much to the teenagers praise.

They all started dancing to the heavy beats and low bass. James shook his head; he didn't know how they listened to this stuff. Grace suddenly appeared next to him. Gone was her costume from before replacing it were faded jeans and a layered long sleeve shirt. The sleeves were pushed up her arms and her silver cross necklace sparkled when the moving lights hit it. Her hair was still curled from before and bounced as she moved to the beat of the music. James noticed this and said.

"Whoa, you like this music?"
Grace didn't answer, she just kept moving along with the song. James rolled his eyes at her.

"Listen," James started again almost having to shout over the music. "I have been wanting to talk to you."
Grace shook her head watching the teens move with the rhythms. She moved toward them and danced along the way.

"Hey, wait, can we talk?" James shouted to her.
"No." She shouted back. "But we can dance!"
Oh no way!

Grace continued to drift toward the dance floor. Then he saw Kathy take Eugene's arm pulling him into the crowd of dancing teenagers. He looked at James with a helpless expression. They too started dancing. Soon Martha had dragged Nelson into the fray.

You've got to be kidding me.

James thought as he reluctantly walked to the others. All the teens saw the adults enter the dance floor and really began moving around excitedly. One boy broke out from the rest dancing his own moves as everyone made a circle around him cheering him on. As he finished his bizarre style of dancing, two girls entered the middle simulating the same moves together right along with each beat. James didn't think they were too bad, as he stood next to Grace motionless. An elbow hit him in the shoulder; he looked over at Grace as she continued to move to the song. Her facial expression was telling him to dance.

Again, he rolled his eyes at her. How in the world was this relaxing for anyone? Actually, James was surrounded by people and he didn't feel overwhelmed. He was a little hot, but no blurry vision or nausea. This made him feel pretty good. He hadn't realized or noticed it before, but he really didn't feel like blacking out at all throughout the whole day. That was until Grace pushed him out in the middle of the circle. Now, he wished that he would drop straight to the ground right then and there. But nothing and the music seemed to get louder and faster.

Then worst of all, everyone started chanting his name. James froze looking at the smiling eager faces that surrounded him. Just then Nelson jumped into the circle with him and froze as well. Back to back, he leaned in next to James' ear and spoke.

"Disco."

James mind was mush. Did he hear Nelson right? It didn't matter, the two men where off and moving. They each pointed down across their bodies and out up over their heads right along with every pound of beat. James was surprised at himself that he could even keep up with the speed of the music. The whole room went wild at them. Then, as if they had been practicing for days, they switched right on cue from disco dancing to the robot.

Moving their joints in a mechanical fashion, slapped hands and stayed right in sequence with the song. Soon everyone had joined in making his or her own ridged movements until the song came to an end. Laughing at themselves and all having a good time, the mood of the dance floor changed when the tall boy, who had been operating the music, put on a much slower tune. James quickly grabbed Grace by the arm as she started to walk off the dance floor.

"I still want to talk to you." He said moving his hand from her arm down to her hand. He spun her around once and placed his other arm on her back, pulling her close to him. Grace reached up with her other hand and put on James' opposite shoulder. She was impressed and breathless by his effortless moves.

"Wow James, you're quite the dancer."

"I like to take it slow."

"Well, you've certainly got the touch."

"My mom taught me to dance, when my dad was away on business trips. She used to put on music after dinner and we would dance half the night."

"I'll have to thank her sometime."James took his eyes off Grace's

"She and my dad both passed away when I was ten."

"Oh, I'm so sorry." Grace felt horrible.

"Thanks, it's ok; it was a long time ago."

He returned his eyes back on her. Grace looked beautiful; the dim glow from the lights above them sparkled in her crystal blue eyes. The others must have been getting restless because the slow song was cut short and on came a rock anthem. The teenagers crowed the floor again dancing with each other. James and Grace parted from each other, but not entirely. They held each other's fingers together, Grace whispered into James's ear.

"Why don't we go for a walk?"

She led him to the entrance door that took them outside.

24

The night was getting darker, but Grace was sure they had some time before the bon fire started. She and James had been walking for while in complete silence. Not that their stroll had become awkward, but just letting each other think for a moment and taking time to get comfortable. Now that the sun had gone down, the cool air of night had very well settled in. It was a refreshing difference from the warm dance floor. A small gust of wind blew along with them, keeping the conditions a bit colder then they had expected. James enjoyed the woods. Being amongst the trees, he felt open and alive. Grace's voice came to him crisp and clear.

"So, what are you thinking about?"

He didn't expect her to start the conversation yet, but he was glad she did because they had a lot to talk about.

"I'm praying." He replied.

"Oh, I'm sorry I'll let you finish."

"No, it ok, I been wanting to talking to you."

"Me too."

"I've found that being out here in the woods and nature help me open my heart. To talk to God and pray to him"

"Like how?" She asked.

"Well, from the talk you gave, it really hit home with me. So, I've been praying to Jesus for forgiveness."

"That's a great place to start." She added now hanging on his every word. "I've been so proud of you this weekend, James. I've seen the Lord grow inside of you and capture your heart."
James shook his head agreeing with her.

"I am becoming a different person." James waited a moment and they stopped walking. "It's because of you Grace." She blushed at the comment. "You've been my inspiration of faith."
Grace thought she could jump and fly amongst the night clouds; she felt so good. She smiled big at him.

They began to walk again and they joined their hands.

"James, do you think there is something going on between us? I mean the events that have happened this weekend, have been really amazing."

James was thinking almost the same thing.

"But, I really don't know who you are?" Grace started to laugh out loud at herself. James stopped walking and released his hand from hers. With a smile on his own face, he said,

"Wait, what's so funny?"
She covered her mouth trying to control her giggles.

"Well, you can start with telling me what did 'slipper mongoose' mean from the relay race?"
She smiled playfully again as did James.

"I'll tell you only if you answer a question I've been racking my brain over ever since I meet you."

"Deal."

"Back in college, we had this professor that taught an advertising class and he keeps telling us to think outside the box when coming up with design proposals. Therefore, a group of us had a project together in his class and we had to come up with a way to sell something outrageous.

We were assigned "The Slippery Mongoose". James laughed a second just remembering the tale.

Grace watched as he told his story. His facial expressions and the emotions in his words told Grace it was a fond memory and that James truly enjoyed telling her about it.

"So all we had for the project was the name, the title of the product. Can you believe it we had to sell something called a 'Slippery Mongoose'?" James shook his head as if he had heard it for the first time. "We had a heck of time trying to 'sell' our product in front of our class, along with keeping straight faces."

They both laughed envisioning the moment.

"So what grade did you end up getting on it?" She asked.

"Oh, I don't even remember, but from then on we all had the joke 'Slippery Mongoose'. We used it for a softball league team mascot, an ultimate Frisbee team name, and even one guy named his local band after it. We all got a kick out of it."

They both laughed some more.

"So, somehow it popped into my head during the race today and I was nervous not knowing the teens in my group yet. I just figured it would get them excited about the relay."

"It was great and a wonderful way to break the ice with them". Grace looked at James. "You see, that is what I mean about God moving inside of you, things like that." He gave her a face of puzzlement.

"You actually remind me a lot of myself when I started LIFT." James had been wondering about LIFT and how it had been started. "I really wasn't someone to be outgoing and involved especially with teens, I essentially fear it."

"I am surprised you say that. You do so well with them."
She thanked him saying,

"I had to do a bunch of praying and soul searching when deciding to create LIFT."

As they walked on, Grace continued to talk about how God had worked through her to overcome her doubts and fears for her to see His path for her life. This made James think about his own life and what kind of path God had designed for him. It was a bit mind blowing for him to comprehend. But he was sure that with Grace's help and support he could find it.

Grace went on telling James about the faithfulness of her mother and she influenced and inspired Grace's own faith in God. How her mother lost her battle with cancer and how she now lived with her father in the country.

James could easily relate to Grace and how she had felt losing a parent at such a young age. Walking hand in hand again, the wind blew at them but didn't discourage their growing connection. They both knew something was uniting them in a relationship beyond their control. Grace didn't want the walk to end. Together they sat down on a small hill that over looked a tiny meadow.

"So, what was it you wanted to ask me?" She asked James. His mind was swirling with so many thoughts at the moment he couldn't think.

"Oh, right, ok. At the base of your business card, you have the letters J M and the number forty-six. What does it stand for?"

Grace threw her head back with laughter, her blonde curly hair floating in the soft wind.

"That's actually a shortened verse from the bible. When I got the cards made, I could only put so many words on it. So, I had to use just two letters and two numbers."

James wished he had brought his bible with him. He so wanted her to point out some direction for him when reading it.

"The book is James, the chapter is four and the verse number is six." James started to understand how the names and numbers went together.

"Remember when you told me your name." James nodded his head.

"And that I started laughing when you said it. It's because of that bible verse. It's a verse my mom gave to me. She told me it was the verse that God gave her when she was pregnant with me. That is why I am named Grace."

"How does the verse go?" He asked curious to hear it.

"But He gives us more grace. That is why Scripture says: "God opposes the proud, but gives grace to the humble.""

James liked it. It described Grace very well.

"That's why I believe you and I have a link James."

"What, because of a bible verse?"

"Well, not only that, but God is showing us something. He is showing us his design on life. How He longs for us, His people, every one of us. If we would just look for the signs in the world around us, we would see His hand working."

"How so?"

"Like life and death. Take my mom for example. She taught me about the Lord and that secured my faith in Him. Everyone around us is a part of that."

James still didn't follow.

"But your mom's cancer wasn't cured. Why didn't God let your mom live?" He asked hoping it wasn't a difficult question for Grace to answer.

"Exactly, I prayed to God everyday after she passed away asking Him the same thing."

"What was His answer?"

"Well, I didn't get the answer right away."

"But the answer came in the form of LIFT. You see, since I had such a grasp on my faith, I could teach others. Maybe my mother had to die to help discover that. Push me to grow and move on."

James' head was twisted with thoughts. How did his parents' death have to do with his own path from God? What was He trying to show James?

"Another example." Grace went on. "How we met, I didn't plan on hitting your car. But I did and look at what came from it."

James knew she was right. If he would have never meet Grace, this whole weekend would have never happened.

"That is why I believe we are meant to be together."

She said and looked up at him. James could see it now. He cared for Grace very much. He had been attracted to her ever since the first time he had laid eyes on her, but he never knew it. God *was* working in his life.

A chill in the air made Grace shutter and she wrapped her arms around herself. James removed his jacket and placed it over her shoulders. He looked into those dazing blue eyes as the moonlight caught her face just right. He took her in his arms, leaned down slowly and pressed his lips against hers. They held together for a second and then parted gradually. The stillness of the moment was invigorating. Grace curled her small mouth into one of her sweet smiles and looked away. James darted his own eyes in the opposite direction. A few minutes passed as they held each other close, the bright stars above shining over them.

James was the first to speak.

"So, what now?"

Grace laughed at his remark.

"Well, we should probably head back to the lodge. I'm sure they're looking for us and ready to start the bon fire."

Grace wished this moment could go on forever, but this weekend wasn't over. They both stood up dusting themselves off and joined hands again turning in the direction of the lodge. But, before they could take one step, Father Warren came into view. His breath visible from the cold, he walked up to the couple.

"Grace, we've been looking for you everywhere." He tried to catch his breath. The man's face looked troubled and stricken with worry.

"Slow down Father, what's the matter?" James asked steadying the man with his arm.

The priest took a deep swallow of air and looked with his large eyes at Grace.

"Grace dear, it's your father." He panted some more. "He's had another stroke."

Grace clutched her arms around James he put his right arm over her body as if protecting her from the news to come.

"He's ok right." Grace asked fearful, her eyes welling up with tears, but still listening.

The old man was downcast sorrowful.

"I'm sorry my dear, he didn't make it."

25

Everyone agreed with Father Warren's decision. Grace needed to return home as quickly as possible. The arrangements had all been worked out between the youth group leaders. Since James had driven his mustang, he would transport Grace back to the city. Their small groups would each be divided up between the other remaining seven. Everything would go along with the rest of the weekend as planned and they all would arrive back in St. Luke's parking lot Sunday afternoon. As the teens gathered outside for the bonfire Grace said her goodbyes to the adults. She felt reluctant to leave them, but her friends reassured that everything would be fine and that she needed to take time to herself. James packed the bags and belongings of both of them into his car and climbed in the vehicle with Grace.

Now as the red mustang traveled down the dark vacant highway in the middle of the night, James and Grace where both lost in each of their own thoughts. The car ride had been silent for almost half an hour as they sped along. James didn't want to disturb Grace as she prayed and took in the reality of her father's death. He snuck a look at her, pretending to adjust the rear view mirror. Though it was dark and hard to make out her beautiful face, James knew she looked miserable. She rested her head against the passenger side window staring up into the sky, as if she was peering in the heavens searching out her father. James hated to see her this way.

He wanted to hold her, tell her everything was going to be ok, take away her hurt and pain. Praying now as well, he asked God to give strength to Grace to make it through this tough ordeal. James knew first hand how hard it was not just to lose one parent, but both. The loneliness, the inescapable depression, the heartache it caused was terrible to bear alone. His thoughts drifted to his own parents. In his newfound faith, he wondered if they were watching over him. Did they approve of his life? His choices? It had been so long ago. The pain of their absence was still inside of him. He so longed to see them. What would his father think of his career? And what about his career? James was still unemployed. The realization of that thought again brought him down. It was easy this weekend to forget about his joblessness, but life hadn't stopped. He hoped to hear back something soon. What if he didn't hear anything? The search would go on. How long would it take? These thoughts started to pull on his emotions. Another possibility was that his perspectives on his career changed. Is this path what God was guiding him to do with his life, advertising and marketing? He thought it's what he wanted as an occupation, yet now he wasn't so sure. His goals had shifted in life. He wanted his new faith and God's plan to rule his way. How was he supposed to define that? The only thing James knew for sure was that he cared deeply for Grace. She had shown him a love that was beyond anything he could imagine. So, how did she fit into his life? Worst yet, he hadn't told Grace any of this. Would she accept his current unemployed status? His mind warped in panic as he gripped the steering wheel in clenched fists. He looked over at her again. The dim glow from the dashboard was about all that he had to reveal her features. James yearned to talk to her about all of his problems. Maybe she would have some ideas for a new career he could pursue or how he could discover himself from the eyes of God using his bible. He talked himself out of the thought. Right now wasn't the time. He felt selfish for thinking of himself. She needed him now, more than ever.

"I'm scared, James." Grace said with her head still resting against the window. Her voice soft, distant, but he could hear her.

"Scared of what Grace?" She was quiet for a moment searching for the right words.

"I'm scared of what will come next. I have no family now." A tear rolled down his cheek.

"That's not true." James said trying to reassure her. "You've got LIFT to support you and I'll be here for you."

She leaned up from the window facing James lovingly.

"And if there's one thing I learned from you this weekend. It's that Jesus will forever be at your side along with a God that loves you very much."

She smiled; James was becoming stronger in his faith faster than she had thought. Again, he reminded Grace of herself, this lifted her spirits a little. Reaching over, she took his free hand and held it in hers. The warming touch and strong grip gave her a silent pulse and comfort.

"Do you want to talk about anything?" James asked rubbing his thumb over the smooth skin of her hand. Grace turned her head away from James looking out into the night. He gave her some space focusing on the road in front of him.

Finally, her voice came back saying,

"After my mom passed away, he became different.

He did a lot of drinking...alone in the basement." Grace wiped a tear from her face.

"He would abuse me, but it wasn't his fault, he was scared like I am scared now."

Tears fell freely from her eyes. Composing herself and wanting to go on, talking through them.

"I lived with my mom's parents until I graduated from college. That's when he had his first stroke and I moved back in with him."

Grace's voice got stronger as she kept remembering. She felt the warming presence of her mother's spirit surround her.

"Then after his second stroke, everybody told me that he wasn't himself, that I should put him into a nursing home."
She shook her head in disagreement.

"I didn't want to lose our home. It was the only thing we had left to remember her by."
She closed her eyes and clutched her silver cross.

"But, now that he's gone, I won't be able to..."
Letting go of James' hand she covered her face breaking down weeping. James felt horrible for her.

"It will be ok Grace, we'll get through this together."
She started to calm down, listening to him.

"We will figure out a way for you to keep your house."

Truth was that James had no idea how they would, but for right now, the idea was making Grace feel better. She used the sleeve of her shirt to wipe her eyes dry. Again, the car became filled with silence. James' thoughts turned to the possibilities of saving Grace's home as they drove on down the freeway.

Off in the distance, James could see the city lights. He had forgotten how they looked compared to the glowing stars that he had seen on his walk with Grace. He already missed the freedom of the woods, the openness of the outdoors. He wouldn't find that type of feeling in the city. But, the mustang wasn't heading to the city. By Grace's direction, they took an exit that led to a small collection of houses just outside the city limits. Further down the dark street, they came to a ranch style brick home with a dark roof. James had a hard time making out anything else, as the car pulled into the cement driveway. He killed the engine and they both just sat for a moment. They were in complete darkness, but James knew something was right with Grace. She acted like she didn't want to go into the house. As if she was afraid of what she might find inside, even though the home was empty. Grace closed her eyes and pushed open the car door. James did likewise grabbing her bag from the back seat. He walked her to the front door. Unlocking it, James handed Grace her bag. Before she took it, she opened her mouth and spoke asking.

"Would you like to come in?"

Grace stood still, looking afraid; he could see it in her eyes. James hesitated a second, but he knew what she was feeling, so he answered saying.

"Yeah, sure."

He kept the bag on his shoulder and entered the house. James wanted to put her mind at ease and help in any way that he could. As he walked through the small foyer, he took in the interior of the home. It was smaller than what he had thought it was when outside. Grace turned on some lights as he looked around. Dropping the bag at his feet, James noticed that the inside was sparsely decorated. Some pictures hung on the wall next to him; he moved closer and inspected them. In a series of three photos, that pictured Grace and her mother, showed how much Grace resembled her.

"Wow, you look just like her." Grace hadn't seen James admiring the pictures. She was too busy making her way to the answering machine in the kitchen. Hoping that they hadn't started, the machine message display read zero. Grace let out a soft sigh and yawned. The clock on the kitchen wall said it was well past two in the morning. The house was so quiet. She walked to her father's room, but didn't go in. Standing in the frame of the doorway, Grace envisioned a younger version of herself and the night her mom died. She could smell his aftershave wafting from the room, as if he was standing in her spot where she stood now, looking on the younger Grace as she prayed over her beloved mother.

A hand on her shoulder made her jump and for a second Grace thought it was her father's. She turned and found James behind her. Grace buried her face in his chest as he wrapped his arms around her. James closed his own eyes and prayed for her. They held close for a while, and then parted when James asked,

"Are you going to be ok?" Grace was quiet. "Let me give my cell number so you can call me when you want me to pick you up in the morning to get your truck from church." She sniffled and cleared her throat, looking up at him with hope in her eyes.

"Could you stay?" James knew Grace needed him. He wanted to give her his help, support...love. Taking a deep breath, he agreed to stay with her and she hugged him again. Grace knew God had put James in her life for a reason. This had to be it. A smile drew across her face.

"You can sleep over there." She pointed to a tan couch. "I'll get you a pillow and some blankets." Grace turned and walked down the hall. Suddenly James started to feel uneasy about staying. What would it be like in the morning? Was this the right thing to do and should he be doing this? Before he could answer himself, Grace had thrust a pillow and blankets into his arms.

"Are you sure this is ok?" She asked. James really wasn't sure, but replied.

"Yeah."
He laid out the pillow and blankets on the couch as Grace asked him if he wanted something to drink.

"Water will be fine." James felt like he needed his own bag so he told her he was going to the car to get it.

She nodded her head and returned to the kitchen for his glass of water and something for herself. When James went back out to the car, he said a prayer of patience, not that he didn't want to be here with Grace, but that it had been a long day and was sure that they both were in need of some serious sleep. Slamming the car door, he hefted his bag onto his shoulder. A slight glimmer caught his eye as James looked up. Although the night air was pretty chilly, he moved in the direction of the light. Around the right side of the house, James found a dark blue lake that shimmered in the reflection of the moon. He hadn't seen it before because they had driven in from the other side of the street. Surrounded among a number of thick trees and even darker forest beyond it, the lake sat motionless. James thought this was great. A quick getaway from the busyness of the city, he could come out here and visit Grace and get his craving of solitude in the woods he so longed for. As he reentered, the house and he felt the warmth tingle his skin. It seemed to be getting colder by the minute out there. James found Grace waiting for him on the couch sipping her own drink. She rose as he came into the living room.

"Great you go your stuff. Please feel free to make yourself at home. The bathroom is right down the hall and my room is the next one down if you need anything." She looked into his eyes and James noted that she seemed to be doing better.

"I'll be fine." He said anxiously. "We both really need some rest." She agreed with him. He set his bag down on the couch and she started for her room.

"James there is one more thing."
He sighed raising his eyebrows ready to listen.

"Do you think we could pray together before we call it a night?"

James smiled at her and they both seated themselves on the couch. They closed their eyes, joined hands and prayed. Grace started. She asked God to have mercy on her father's soul and give him peace, then she asked Jesus to surround her with love and support through this trying time. Lastly, Grace prayed in thanksgiving for James and how God had captured his heart, and for God to show him all the love and meaning in his life that God had shown her. Then James began his prayer. He was cautious at first, but prayed for Grace's father and for her well-being. Going on about how much he had learned the past weekend and how he wanted God and Jesus in his life. As Grace did, James prayed for their relationship and to guide them down the life He had set for them. After James had finished, Grace squeezed his hands and opened her eyes. She stood to go to her room. In self-confidence, James spoke lovingly to her saying.

"I am right here."

Grace's heart beat with affection like no other and she kissed him lightly on cheek.

Then she placed her hand over his chest where his heart was located.

"I am right here."

She bounded off to her room and left James to himself.

But, James didn't sleep; instead he produced his black leather bible from his bag. Opening it to the page that he had cornered from before and read deeply until the sun came up.

26

Frank Connelly's funeral was on the following Tuesday at St. Luke's. It had been a long time since James had been to a funeral, but he was surprised at the turnout of the event. Despite the declining warmth of the weather, so many people came to give their condolences such that the visitation lasted beyond the allotted time. Most of the attendees were there because they knew Grace some how and wanted to support her through the loss. Although a large number of them left when the funeral service started, the church was still packed as the ceremony began. The service was short, but James thought Father Warren's eulogy was respectful and fulfilling in Grace's father's memory. It was decided that a burial service would be done privately and later on in the week.

A small gathering at Grace's home in the country followed the memorial service. All of the youth group adult leaders, Father Warren, and some of the schoolteachers, who had helped with the retreat, were present. It was nice for Grace to be surrounded by her loved ones. She really needed the comfort. Ever since the night James had stayed over, Grace had become very depressed and unconnected.

Quite the opposite of what he was expecting, from her. That Sunday, Grace, never showed up for the LIFT youth night. Nobody discussed it and went on with the night's activities. But, when one absence from Sunday youth group nights turned into two, it became something different. Nobody had made contact with her for the past two weeks. A couple of teachers were switching back and forth covering her religion class. Everyone wanted to let Grace cope in her own way, give her time to recollect herself.

That had been over two weeks ago and James hadn't talked to or seen Grace since after her father's funeral. Flipping again through his bible seated on this kitchen table, his cell phone next to him, he was starting to getting worried about her. Thomas had gotten in touch with James the week before and since James had canceled the first dinner, they had set up another get together for tonight. He didn't want to let his uncle down again. In addition, he wanted Thomas to meet Grace. Not just that James sought to see her again as well.

Just call her. He thought. Maybe she was waiting for him to? Emotionally or physically, would she be ready to go out, especially, meeting people she didn't know yet? The whole thing would be a bad idea. No, James would just go by himself, alone, and have dinner with his Uncle, Thomas, and Jan. Possibly he could give Grace a call after the meal. Maybe she would invite him over and they could talk. Yeah, he would like that.

Something had prompted him to stop and read the page he had stopped on in the bible. As he became glued to the passage, James' cell phone rang out. He jumped with surprise. Shaking his head and gripping the phone in his hands, checked the caller ID. Unexpectedly, it was Grace calling him. A smile came across his face as he flipped open the device.

"Hello."

"Um, Hi."

Silence fell over him, it was wonderful to her hear voice. He quickly thanked God in his mind and then Grace's voice came again.

"Listen, I am really sorry, James. I know I have been really distant with everyone lately. I hope you're not angry with me."

He shook his head as if she could see his answer. Then he said it.

"No, don't worry, nobody is upset with you. We all understand what you are going through." He took a breath, still relieved to be listening to Grace's voice and went on;

"I...we got nervous when we didn't hear from you for two weeks. We just wanted to support you in anyway that we can."

There was a short pause on the other end of the line.

"Thank you, James." She said sincerely. "And don't worry, I plan on calling everyone and letting them know that I am ok. I just need some time to sort some things out."

Thoughts of how much Grace was worried about losing her house ran through James' mind.

"And did you?" He asked.

"Yes I did and I am satisfied with my decisions. God has been a large part of that."

James smiled again knowing that Grace would never waiver her commitment to her faith.

"Well, if you would like my help on anything just say the word." Grace giggled a bit on the other line.

"Actually, I want to see you. I really missed you."

"I missed you too."

Both of them released a brief exhale of breath, as if it was all they needed to hear from one another.

"Grace, I understand if you don't feel up to it and I know it's the spur of the moment, but I'm having dinner tonight with my Uncle and his new fiancé. Would you like to join us?"

"Oh, yes that would be fantastic." She said eagerly, unable to hold back her excitement. James checked his watch, the time read almost two in the afternoon.

"Great, Thomas made reservations around six at Crystal Lake Country Club. I am not sure if you have been there before, but it's kind of classy. Just so you know how to dress, I will be wearing a suit jacket and a tie."
Grace giggled again.

"What? Yes, I own a tie. Is that so hard to believe?"
She snickered some more.

"It's really great to talk to you again James."

"Yeah, I can't wait to see you tonight. Hey, I can pick you up if you want me to."
Grace agreed to his offer. They both said goodbye and hung up.

James closed his eyes, grinning wide and whispered a prayer of thankfulness and praise.

Opening his eyes and wiping his face dry with a cloth towel, looked at his clean-shaven reflection in the bathroom mirror. After doing some cleaning and running a few errands, James showered and now had just finished shaving as he continued to ready himself for his dinner engagement. He walked to his closet and thumbed through his collection of long neckties. He wanted one that would match perfectly with his outfit. Pulling a silk royal blue Italian made selection from the group, he held the garment against his light colored button down shirt and returned to the mirror. James loosely draped the top over his chest adding the tie and made the decision to go with the choice. He wanted to look his best for Grace. Going back to his closet, he grabbed the black slacks that coordinated with the jacket and slipped them on. Hoping he had enough time stop before he made it to Grace's house to purchase some flowers for her, he whipped on a black leather belt, tucked in his shirt and did up his pants.

Once more in front of the mirror, James drew the long tie around his collar. He was so excited that he had to stop a minute and remember how to knot the expensive accessory. Lastly, he retrieved his leather shoes and stepped into them to complete his ensemble. James checked the time to make sure he was allowing enough time to make it all the way out to Grace's house and then on to Crystal Lake. He had more than enough. That was good thing; James liked to be on time. He was done with running late and having to come up with lies and excuses. This was the new James, more confident, relaxed, moral, and on time.

From the hall closet, he grabbed his wool coat, the weather called for below freezing temps and possible rain. A loud ringing sounded out from his pants pocket. He recognized it as his cell phone; James was receiving an incoming call. Removing the cell from his pocket flipped it open.

It had to be Grace. James thought, but was shocked when the caller ID read a different number.

"Hello?"

"James, hey what's up? It's Bart. Listen I've got some great news." James was totally thrown off; he didn't expect a call from Bart.

"Remember I told you that you were taking a longshot at the Baxter position? Well, when I put a call into a guy I know that works there it paid off. Get this, Baxter himself and a couple of his colleagues will be in town next month. My guy gave them your resume and they said they would like to get in touch with you while in town."

James was reeling from the news he had just heard. Was this really happening? He didn't know what to say.

"James?"

"Yeah, I'm here. Man, this is big."

"You betcha, but be ready, somebody from Baxter's office will be contacting you soon. They'll probably want to set up a meeting time and place."

"Wow, Bart I don't know how to thank you."

"No need just remember me when you're on the top, buddy."

They both had a laugh and said goodbye. James had to reconnect with reality. He couldn't stop the grin from spreading across his face. Blinking his eyes regained his original purpose.

Satisfied that he had all that he needed before he left his condo, he closed and locked the door. Turning down the hall, he walked to the elevators stopping in front of them. James took a deep swallow and pressed the down button. He reminded himself of his self-assurance and stood firm. The elevator was taking a long time and James started eyeing the door that led to stairs.

It would be quicker. He reasoned. *No, I've got plenty of time.* Again, he gathered inner strength and readied himself for the dinner with Grace and the others. Tonight was going to be a huge step for James and he was prepared for it. He and Thomas had to come to a reckoning of their relationship together. James wanted to be completely honest with the man. He would have to swallow his pride and do what was best for his future. He couldn't be unemployed for the rest of his life. But, now with the news of an upcoming interview with Baxter Advertising, James felt more sure of his potential employment. And what of his relationship with Grace? If they ever wanted to pursue more than just a couple, he would have to support her. James couldn't believe he was even thinking about marriage being a possibility with her, but something was tugging at his soul, something wildly unimaginable had happened to his life through Grace and he wanted to spend the rest of his life with her.

If now he could just get past his fear and ride the elevator, he could get on with the night's event. The elevator pinged and the metal doors slid open revealing an empty lift. It came as a spot of relief as he walked into the elevator. The doors slid and locked into place behind him. There was no escape now, no way out. A small panic broke through his thoughts and he silenced it with a prayer. Tapping the ground floor button, the lift clunked, shifted, and began on it decent. James checked his distorted image in the silver door in front of him. His face looked like his stomach felt. He took his coat, which had been folded over his left arm, opened it up, and slipped it on. Before he knew, he had arrived. The metal doors wheeled open and James stood looking out amongst the lobby. Astonished that the ride had been so quick, he stepped out of the elevator. He looked over his shoulder and watched the doors again slide closed. A small click announced that it was on its way to pick up another passenger. James pumped both of his fists into the air and howled in bliss. A woman who was walking from a row of mailboxes gave him an awkward look. James just smiled at what he had just achieved.

A light flaky snow blew through the evening air. Exiting the side door that opened to the parking lot, James was surprised to see the dusty white.

Snow in late October?

The local weather had called for rain, but it must have been colder than they thought. James was glad he had his coat with him and hoped Grace dressed warm enough. Clicking his garage door opener, he walked to his beloved classic car and entered the driver side. James backed the vehicle out slowly; as he did, he noticed his landlord throwing some trash away in the condo's dumpster.

"Hey Burt how's it going?" James hollered to him through the open passenger window.

Burt turned around and saw James' mustang. The husky man wore a blue jogging tracksuit with white strips down the length of the arms and legs, the collar flipped up, his hands deep in his pockets. His bad comb-over wafted in the wind as he walked up to the mustang.

The man waved his pudgy fingers and then stopped dead in his tracks. Staring at the back end of the red mustang, Burt pointed at it saying.

"Whoa, Mr. Mason looks like somebody got you good." The landlord was indicating the green scar from Grace's truck.

"I know, isn't it great?" James replied.
He gave Burt a wave back and sped from the lot and onto the street. The landlord stood opened mouth slightly shaking his head at James.

"It must be the cold weather!" The man thought out loud.

Having been through five outfits already, she was sure this was the one. Grace took one last glance in the mirror at her rich blue sparkling dress and was glad that it still fit her. It been so long since she had dressed up so nice just to go on a date; besides, when was the last time she had been on a real date? Was it with Nelson? She forgot the thought and smoothed her dress down her hips.

Turning around and looking over her shoulder, she checked the back of the garment for the third time.

Grace, just finish getting ready, he'll be here any minute.

She told herself. Flipping open a small wooden box, she picked out a pair of silver earrings. They had been her mothers. Grace really wasn't someone who wore a lot of jewelry, except her cross necklace of course, but as she applied the earrings she wished that she had more often.

She liked the way they looked on her. Grace wanted to look nice for James and hoped his uncle liked her.

Excited about the night out, she wanted to escape the house a bit; the last two weeks had been tiring for her.

Grace had to make a lot of decisions during them. Not just things that had to do with her dad's passing, but questions and feelings she had personally. Grace wanted to be on the correct path that fulfilled God's plan for her. Through it all, for a moment, she just wanted to give up, just collapse and fall into her depressed mentality. Having James stay over the first night was a blessing and although he had been so charming, he didn't understand then what she was going through. Everyone was being so helpful and caring and it was all very sweet, but this had happened before to

Grace and while it was great to have everybody, she still felt alone. Determined not allow the depression get the best of her, she just needed to have some time to herself and God. But, getting out tonight with James was also just what she wanted. Take a break from the choices and mind raking thoughts, and relax; maybe learn more about James through his uncle. It would certainly be interesting to see what the man was like. Suddenly the doorbell rang, the noise startled Grace and she moved from her small vanity in her room. Racing to the front door, took a quick breath and opened it. There he stood on the front step a bundle of beautiful flowers in hand, dressed attractively in a tailored suit and tie. The Snow floated around James reflected the light like small growing lights. She was breathless for him. Grace took the arranged bouquet of flowers and smelled them. She invited him in while she went to find a vase to put the bouquet in. Returning to the small foyer they both stood in quiet stance. They couldn't take each others eyes off the vision before them, it felt like a high school dance or something juvenile like that. But, it wasn't; this was a real date with an amazing man. He spoke first.

"Grace...you look...exquisite." She blushed at the statement.

"Well, certainly clean up nice as well."

"What... this only took five minutes." He said playfully.

"Oh, it only took me four and I even had time to change my shoes." They both laughed, Grace was glad for this. It felt wonderful to be with James.

"Are you ready to go? We'd better get moving if we are going to make it on time with this snow."

"Can you believe this weather?"
James shook his head with another smile, still glancing over Grace.

"I am afraid I don't have my winter coat though." She bit her lower lip and raised her eyebrows.

"Ok, that's no problem. I've got one right here." James removed his wool coat as Grace turned her back to him. He placed the garment over her bare shoulders. The touch of his hands sent goose bumps over her skin. She missed James more than she had thought. He walked Grace out to the still running Mustang, opened the passenger door and let her in. Grace could get used to this kind of treatment, flowers, offering his coat, opening her door for her. But it weren't just those things, Grace really felt connected to James. Moreover, he looked fantastic in that suit. James climbed in the driver seat and buckled his seatbelt.
He looked at Grace.

"Are you ready for this?" Grace wasn't sure what he meant by that, did he mean tonight or to spend the rest of their lives together. She responded yes, secretly to both.

27

Crystal Lake Country Club was about a good half hour from Grace's house in the country. Therefore, James and Grace had some time to talk. Grace first explained to James that she had come to the conclusion to sell her parents country home. After numerous prayers and fighting inner emotions, she decided it would be the best thing to do. Grace had to move on with her life. James complimented her on her tough decision then he gave her his big news. Returning to the day that he met Grace when they had the accident, he described his emotions that day, explaining to her how he was fired from Kruger and Sons.

James went on to telling her that he was currently unemployed. It was harder to say the words than he thought. However, just as it was her nature, Grace received his humiliation with compassion. Again, James was reminded of the powerful influence Grace's presence had on him. Her precious smile captured his heart and calmed his soul. Keeping with the conversation, next told her about his opportunity for employment through an interview next month. Grace was thrilled at the possibility for him and his budding career. Then she asked a question James wasn't quite prepared for. She asked if it was what God was leading him to do. James steadied his focus on the semi-slick road before him. It was an honestly good question that took James a minute to contemplate. It hadn't occurred to him to pray about his new endeavor. What was God's plan for his career? Was this interview a sign of the right direction? It had to be why else would he have been offered it? James kept these thoughts to himself. Grace didn't push the idea further. It was in God's hands and He would make all things good. Changing the subject, Grace asked about Thomas. Still on thoughts of the upcoming interview, James had to rip his mind back to the present. Grace had opened a whole new set of questions that James would have to review later. Answering her question about Thomas with a flashback in his head, James told her again about his parent's fateful death, and how his uncle Thomas raised him from then on. His values and morals that were instilled in him when he was so young and how they grew as he matured into an adult. James described the difference between him and the other kids of his own age. Not that Thomas had done a bad job in raising James; just that he was a reluctant parent and hadn't planned on rearing a child as his company grew by leaps and bounds. He had always been the corporate superior rather than a father figure. Grace understood as she explained her own childhood with her grandparents, and how her own father treated her. Something she forgave the man for long ago. James tried to remember if he had ever forgiven Thomas for his actions. Grace went on talking about her beloved mother, and how she was such a beckon of light in her faith. James was glad that he and Grace had this kind of relationship. The openness and un-daunting attitude drew them together.

The Crystal Lake Country Club came into view. Even though the snow still fell outside, the night was clear, cold, but clear as if snow was just artificially added to the evening to give it a sparkling appearance. The snow, as well, didn't stop others from attending dinner at the country club either. The parking lot was quite full. Yet, James didn't worry about finding a spot even if all the parking space was hosted. As the mustang pulled up to the front entrance, a parking attendant on each side of the car opened the doors. The attendant on the driver side handed James a small ticket with a number printed on it. He shoved it into his pocket and joined Grace who was slightly giggling to herself. The red mustang sped off and James followed it a second and then returned his attention back to Grace.

"What's so funny?" She shook her head and covered her mouth trying to keep in her laughter.

"Never in my life have I been escorted from a vehicle." It was nothing new to James, he had been to Crystal Lake several times and was used to the treatment here. They entered the glowing yellow foyer and another country club employee took James' coat that was over Grace's shoulders and handed James another ticket. Amused again with the good management of the club, Grace jabbed an elbow at James who was smiling now along with her; then she asked,

"How many of those tickets are you going to collect by the end of the night?" James chuckled at the amusing question. He actually hadn't been to Crystal Lake for a while. The country club was members only and Thomas was an elite with their association, but he was the only available way James could enter the establishment. A thin man in short mustache, wearing a tuxedo, hair slicked back, greeted James and Grace.

"Good evening sir and madam, welcome to Crystal Lake Country Club." His hands were clasped behind his back and he stood upright as if he were their personal attendant.

"May I see your membership card or the name of the member you are here to accompany?" James said his uncle's name and the man instantly knew the name and told them to follow his lead.

The dinning hall was a short way down a marble hallway. The group came to a heavily decorated set of double doors. An employee saw them coming and reaching out, he grabbed the brass handle opened the right side for them. The room had high vaulted ceilings, decorated similar to the entrance doors they just came through. About thirty round tables crowded together seated with patrons, filled half the room. No empty table was in sight. The second half was dedicated to a flat marble dance floor, which had a few couples moving to a light string instrument band off to the left of the dance floor. Grace was not laughing now; she was impressed, overtaken by the design of the dinning room. She was also glad there was a dance floor; she had been longing to dance with James again. The tuxedo guide brought them to a round table and sat them down with another couple. Grace assumed that the couple was James' uncle and his fiancé. The man was older than Grace had envisioned, but he was certainly a handsome man. No gray hair indicating his age and he dressed as if he owned the place. Jan was petite woman with short dark brown hair; she too was attractive, possibly a bit younger than the man was in age. She wore an elegant black dress that sparkled with silver shimmering through out, a multi-diamond necklace and ring to match. Grace suddenly felt underdressed, thinking back to another dress that she should have worn instead of her current one. Something about her made Grace recognized Jan, as if she seen the woman before in another life. Everyone greeted each another and made introduction. Jan gave Grace a funny look as they shook hands and then seated themselves at the table. Grace knew this woman before, somewhere.

"I am so glad you guys could make it. We didn't count on this irregular snow." Thomas said.

James and Grace both agreed.

"Jan and I have been looking forward to this for some time."

Jan spoke up saying.

"Oh, James I've heard so much about you, it's great to finally meet you."

"Now, wait a second, have those been good things or bad things Thomas was telling you about me?" Everyone laughed at the table. Thomas was displaced by James' humor and something seemed different about his nephew. A waiter came to the table dressed in a white vest and ties and asked for their beverage selections. After gathering them, the finely dressed waiter gave them the evening's three specials, and then left the table to let them decide their entries. Two of them Grace had never heard of and the third was duck, Grace never tasted duck before and wasn't about to start tonight. Instead, she looked over the menu in front of her. James saw Grace's eyes give away her expression when she heard the specials from the waiter. He hoped all of this wasn't too overwhelming for her. Leaning over and whispering to her he said.

"Don't look at the prices just get something that you will like. I want you to be relaxed and stress free tonight."

Grace gave him a smile in reply. As he looked over his own menu, Thomas asked,

"So, how did you two meet?"

James and Grace looked at each other, both reliving the moment of the car crash in their own minds. James spoke up.

"Well, quite by accident."

Grace let out a shy smirk then explained to James' uncle and Jan how she had sideswiped his mustang. Thomas threw his head back with laughter, slapping James on the shoulder.

"You mean this is Grace, the one whose license you stole the day we meet for lunch?"

James nodded.

"Wait, you stole her driver's license?" Jan chimed in.

"That was somewhat a long day for me and I didn't steal her license, we accidentally switched them." James added.

Finally, it clicked with Thomas in his mind, that day must have been the day James was let go from Kruger. This was something he wanted to address with James. Thomas was worried for his nephew's career status and well-being; yet tonight, James seemed fine. Maybe it was because he had meet Grace. That was the way it was for him when he met Jan.

"So, now you know our story, tell us how you guys met each other." James asked.

Jan opened her mouth to answer, but was cut short as the waiter returned to the table and asked for everyone's order. They went around the table and announced their order, Thomas was last, he also asked for a bottle of wine from the house list.

"Very good sir." The waiter replied snapping his leather notebook closed and leaving them again.

A short silence came over the table and then Jan started to speak again.

"Ok, our story is a bit like yours, wrong place right time, if you know what I mean." James and Grace listened with pleasure.

"I was volunteering down at the soup kitchen one day and just as I was leaving to get into my car, a mugger held me up at knife point."

Grace covered her mouth in astonishment.

"Oh my goodness." She said.

"Oh, don't worry. Your uncle here...uh...Thomas saw the crime and stopped it."

Thomas barraged into the conversation saying.

"I was on my way home from the office and I decided to take a different way home and went by the soup kitchen at just the right time. I pulled my car into the parking lot and honking my horn scared the mugger off. Then stayed with her until police came."

Jan cut back in.

"Then, Thomas was kind enough to follow me home and see me to my front door."

"Wow   that   is   some   story."

"I know we love to tell it." She smiled at Grace.

That is when Grace's memory picked up where she knew Jan from. Even though Grace had been to the soup kitchen many times, it wasn't there that she knew her from. It was St. Luke's.

"Excuse me, but if you don't mind my asking, do you attend St. Luke's church?"

Jan's mouth went wide and she blinked her eyes.

"Oh, now I know where I've seen you before Grace." Obviously, the same thought connected in her mind as well. "Yes, I do attend St. Luke's when I can, but I have been so busy lately with work, I haven't been going to St. Steven's up on Second Street."

The two women laughed with a giddy sound. James and Thomas just shook their heads, smiles on their faces.

The waiter arrived again at the table, a bottle of wine in one hand and four glasses in the other. He poured the wine to each of them and left the bottle, then quickly announced that their meals would be out shortly.

"So, James..." Thomas said turning to James after he had taken a sip of wine. "How is work going?" He asked him directly.

James finished taking a drink from his own glass and swallowed deeply. This was it. What was he going to tell his uncle? He could just skip the part about how he had been fired from Kruger and tell Thomas about his future dealings with Baxter Advertising. He didn't know what to say.

Oh Lord, please help me.

Suddenly, Grace spoke up.

"James they are playing a great song."

James shot Grace a confused look.

"If you guys don't mind, he promised me a dance and I want to make sure that I get it."

Grace stood and grabbed James' arm and practically yanked him from his own seat.

"Sure, by all means a girl's got to get what she wants right." Jan said jokingly.

For some reason, Grace thought she knew that Jan understood what she was doing. Grace liked her. Continuing to tug James along toward the dance floor, she spoke softly into his ear.

"Just promise me that you will talk to Thomas before you go to that interview."

James followed Grace's actions now; she was making a distraction for him to avoid his conversation about his employment with Thomas. They slowly started to move to the music and James thanked God for Grace's quick thinking.

"I promise I will and thank you." He whispered back to her as the danced through the song.

When they were seated back at their table, everyone's dinner had arrived. The conversation about James' job never came back up and he didn't prompt it to either. Thomas and Jan talked a lot about the upcoming spring wedding they were to have next year. How all the decisions and arrangements were driving them crazy. They also mentioned that the church, St. Steven's, wasn't available on the date they desired. Grace offered St. Luke's as a second option. Jan agreed with her that it was their second choice, but hadn't made any reservations yet. Then Grace told them she would be more than happy to inquire for them since she worked there. That's when she described her position at the church and the youth group LIFT. Again, Thomas' mind retraced old thoughts of James talk about the youth group retreat he had taken. He asked James about it and he gladly told his uncle it had been a turning point in his life. The rest of the night went on with great joy and to James luck and surprise, not another word about his employment.

      With the bottle of wine finished between the four of them and the hour growing late, they all decided to retire. Although James and Grace declined, Thomas paid the evening's bill and left a hefty tip with the waiter. Everyone reclaimed their garments at the coat check and awaited each of the vehicles.

As the cold wind whipped at them, they quickly said their goodbyes and headed home.

28

It was later on during week that James intended to keep the promise he had made to Grace. He had to. Not just to honor the promise, but talking with his uncle for his own sake as well. They had much to discuss together. James also wanted Thomas to be the first to see his new purchase and get the man's opinion.

James checked his watch; it was just before seven in the evening as he pulled into Thomas' apartment complex. Calling it an apartment was an understatement. The building was more like the white house and his uncle's apartment could be put in the category of small house. James parked his car and walked to the lobby. A door attendant held open the door for James and gave him a small nod. Stepping into the lobby, it seem as though James had just walked into a five star hotel. A beautiful water fountain, complete with fish in it, trickled quietly to his left, a roaring fireplace surrounded by couches was next to it. That is where he found Thomas. Holding a newspaper open in front of his face, waiting patiently. James called out to his uncle as he made his way toward him. Thomas looked up from his paper and flashed a smile; he checked the watch on his wrist.

"Hey, you're right on time."

James spread a half smile.

"Come on we'll go up stairs and I'll show you around my new place." Thomas rose from the leather couch and led James to a set of elevators. James thought his heart skipped a beat when he saw them. Recently, he had gotten used to the elevator in his own building, but had not ridden any other.

It shouldn't be any different. He reassured himself. Maybe more nice, more open than his and it certainly was as the two men stepped aboard. Thomas pressed the button marked five then turned to James asking.

"Have you eaten yet? I can have something brought up."

This place is like a hotel.

James replied that he had already eaten and thanked Thomas for the offer. They rode the rest of the way in silence. The doors slid open and Thomas walked off the lift and down the long hallway before them. The floor was carpeted and small lights indicated different rooms. James thought the lights looked like something you would put on the outside of your house. Plucking out a set of keys from his pocket Thomas jingled them around his fingers. It was something small, but something James never saw his uncle do before. There was a different kind of air about the man. A bounce in his step, a joy in his voice when he spoke, what was it that had made him this way? James pondered the thought as his cell phone on his hip rang loudly. Thomas stopped before a set of double doors and using a key from the ring in his hand, unlocked the door on the right. Quickly James fumbled for his phone and checked the caller ID. He didn't clearly recognize the number that flashed across the tiny screen. A jolt of consideration crossed his mind.

It could be someone from Baxter Advertising trying to get in touch. James looked up at his uncle, who stood in the doorway to his apartment, waiting for James to enter.

"Go ahead and answer it, it's Grace isn't it?" Thomas raised his eyebrows trying to shuffle James into the living space. James had to take this call, if his hunch was right about this caller being someone from Baxter, then it was the call of a lifetime.

Just answer it. He demanded to himself. Unclipping the phone, James flipped it open and entered his uncle's apartment.

His uncle's apartment was very open, large. Long slender, very artistic windows were paneled on the far wall. They overlooked the wide grounds of the complex. The whole place was decorated in very high taste and expensive items. From the pots and pans hanging over the giant kitchen to the original paintings that graced the interior living room and hallway walls. Finally, James turned his thoughts from his uncle's amazing dwelling to the phone call at hand.

"This is James." The voice on the end of the line identified himself as none other than Baxter's personal assistant. James was just about to leap into the air with joy. Instead, he kept his distance from his uncle. The assistant on the other end told James that Mr. Baxter and some of his associates would be in his area within the next few weeks and they wanted to have interview with James. Inconspicuously, James answered that he would be ready and asked when and where they wanted to meet. The assistant gave James the time, date, and place. Then with that, he said thank you to the man and they both hung up. James kept the phone open against his ear. He was in a bit of shock to all that had just happened. He is about to have an interview with Baxter himself, an opportunity of a lifetime to have a career that would make his dreams come true.

"Who was that?" Came Thomas' voice from across the room.

James froze. What was he going to say to him? This was a topic that he wanted to talk to his uncle about tonight. Why not just tell him? He would be so proud at James' accomplishment,

Thomas might not even care that he had been fired from Kruger.

"Actually..." James started returning the phone to the clip on his belt and moving closer to his uncle.

"Was it someone from Baxter's office?" Thomas asked.

James' mouth hung open at the question. A realization of somewhat buzzed through his mind. All James could say without yelling it was "What?"

"Pretty exciting, isn't it? You see when I found out you had been let go from Kruger. I got in touch with a few of my contacts and had them send me any available positions in advertising." James was blown away by this revelation. Thomas continued explaining the rest of his actions taken on behalf of his nephew.

"Then I thought of Baxter Advertising. The big guy owed me a favor and I gave him a call, he said he wouldn't have any problem giving you a position in his company."
Again James was slammed by Thomas' confession.

"I am sure Grace will be thrilled when you tell her." Thomas stood in front of him with smiles across his face. James just shook his head, trying to collect his thoughts together. Finally putting his thoughts into words, he said;

"So, you knew the whole time about how I had been fired from Kruger?" Thomas nodded.

"Yeah and actually I wasn't sure how I was going to get your resume to Baxter without you knowing. But, you seem to have some contacts of your own."
James pointed an angry finger at his uncle, catching the man off guard.

"And you put me on the fast track to getting the job when they got my resume didn't you?"

"Of course, hey, I thought I was doing you a favor?" Thomas raised his hands in innocence.

"I never asked for your involvement in my career, I can do it on my own. Remember that is something that YOU taught me."

"Listen James I just..."

"No Thomas YOU listen. My whole life you have been raising me to become your corporate partner. Did you ever think that maybe that isn't what I wanted to do?" James was almost shouting now. "I never asked for this life." James turned from his uncle and looked out a window that looked deep into the night sky.

"James, I never asked for this life either. But, I did the best with what I could. After your parents' death, it wasn't easy for me as well."

Calming down a little now, James turned back and faced his uncle.

"Grace already knows about Kruger and Baxter and she is very supportive through anything that might come our way. That weekend retreat that I went on was because of Grace. She invited me along and showed me the true meaning of what it was to have faith in God." Thomas stood listening attentively. "Something changed inside of me and made me look at my life differently."

"I understand what you are saying. After I meet Jan and got to know who she was. It made me look back on my life. She keeps her family so close to her. You're all the family that I have James. After I proposed to her, I wanted to get back in touch with you and regain what we had broken."

James was starting to see Thomas' thinking.

"When I found out you lost your career, I wanted to help in anyway that I could. I guess I should have come to you first."

Taking in a breath of air, James refocused on the conversation. He realized now, Thomas' new mentality, why the man was acting out of character. He was in love. James could easily relate to his uncle's feelings. The relationship James had with Grace was far beyond anything he had ever believed in.

"I'm sorry Thomas, for yelling at you, I really didn't mean what I said. You did a great job raising me. Neither of us were ready for something like that, but we did the best we could, out of love."

Thomas smiled at his nephew and was proud of him. James stuck out his hand and Thomas took it squeezing it in admiration.

"There is just one more thing I've been wanting to ask you James."

James stood ready for his uncle's question.

"Will you be my best man?"

James agreed whole-heartedly bringing the man in closer for a hug. Years of pent up emotion and fears melted away with the strong embrace. They patted each other's back and released, stepping back a moment, smiles on their faces. They both laughed.

"Ok, then." Thomas said. "Tell me more about this Grace."

James explained how God had worked in their lives, brought them together, and how much they were committed to each other. Then, James took out the small box and showed his uncle his recent purchase. Thomas was pleased with James and felt as though he were a son.

29

For the past three weeks, James and Grace had been meeting for bible study at Grace's soon to be sold country home. Every Thursday, the couple would get together and discuss certain topics in the bible or thoughts that they had roaming in their minds. But this Thursday, James hadn't showed up yet. Grace checked the clock for the tenth time; the hands read a quarter to seven. James was forty-five minutes late. She looked at the empty plate in front of her. The meatloaf on the table was cold as was the rest of the food she had prepared for them. Six times she had called his cell phone. No answer every time. She left six voice messages.

Was it the weather? The forecast had called for a blizzard tonight. Grace rose from her seat at the table and peered out through one of her front windows. Nothing but a dark, desolate, night sky looked back. She spoke a breath of prayer, then out of the darkness came a pair of headlights.

Was it James? It had to be. The bright lights came closer and then passed steadily rolling down the country road. Grace's hope sank and she left her spot at the window. Clearing the table of the two place settings and the rest of the meal, she suddenly lost her appetite. Grace returned to the kitchen table and opened her bible. Spreading out some question she had written down for their discussion, she looked them over. Involuntarily, her eyes found the clock on the wall again.

What could he possibly be doing and not call her to say he would be late or worse, not be coming at all. There was only one thing for certain in Grace's head that stood out; and it was that tomorrow was James's big interview with Baxter Advertising. Every time they had spoken, James brought it up. Grace was quite tired of hearing about it and would be glad when it was over. She hoped it was where God was leading James' career. When she had asked him if he had prayed on the decision, he had avoided the question and over time Grace dropped the idea.

Now, as the time reached eight o'clock, Grace gave up on James' arrival and decided to finish up some of her packing. Her childhood home had only been on the market for two weeks before an elderly couple made an offer on it. Grace meet the pair and they seemed very nice, they were looking for a house in the country that they could retire in and when Grace's property came up, they walked through it that same week. Calling it a "perfect fit" they put money down and Grace accepted the offer, all during that week. It had happened so fast. Grace truly didn't mind she wanted to sell the house and was glad it had sold. But this whole week she had been packing her possessions; it was harder than she thought. This house had so many memories. A loving family once lived here for many years and called it their home. That family as gone now and it was heart wrenching for Grace to go through. Once in a while, she would come across long forgotten items or old photos that resurfaced as she pack them away lovingly. She had made her way through the most part of the house. But, she still had the basement to do and wanted to save her parents room for last. Grace took the stairs down to the basement. The lower level had never been finished. The floor was still concrete and the most of the piping still exposed. All it was used for was a place for her father to go and be by himself. She found a handmade workbench cluttered with rusty tools. A worn and faded easy chair and small television set. How long had it been since she had been down here? She hadn't been here when the realtors walked through the house, she wondered what they had thought when they came down here. Grace walked to the workbench. She really had no use for the tools or the musty armchair. Then she spotted a small fridge behind the stairs. Grace knew very well what went on down here years ago. Her father would disappear down in the basement after work for hours at times. That's why she had not been in the basement for so long, Grace didn't dare relive the memories that came flooding back. Chills ran down her body, it was probably because the room wasn't heated, but yet the feelings of loneliness crept up on her. A small cracked framed photo of her parents, several years old, was covered by some paper towels. She took the photo in her hands. Tears welled up in her eyes as thoughts of lost love overtook her emotions. Grace felt abandoned by everyone and now James too. She missed her parents so much. Her body collapsed into the armchair as wet tears dripped down her face.

Where was God in all of this? Grace felt forsaken by Him as well. It wasn't like her to think like this. God had been the only constant in her life. How could she give up on Him now? The emotional rollercoaster her life had taken in the last month had become more than she could handle. So much loss around her, the passing of her father and her tough decision to sell the house, she just couldn't do this anymore. And what about James? Their relationship had grown so close and loving. It had become something that she never thought it would and she wanted to be excited for where it might lead. Where was their future headed? Where was James anyway? This interview had been overtaking his life.

Then Grace heard a sound from above her, footsteps.

It was James. It had to be. She picked her self up from the chair and turned to the stairs. While climbing the steps, she tried to clear her eyes of tears. Just as she reached the top she spotted him. James stood in the foyer with his cell phone pressed to his ear, trying to wiggle free of his coat. He was talking into the device, but Grace couldn't make out the conversation or whom he was talking with. James quickly wrapped up the phone call and finished removing his coat, then flopped it on the tan couch. Reaching down by the door from a spot hidden from Grace's view, he drew out a large black portfolio brief case. James sat down on the couch and unzipped the giant case and flipped through to first page and made a few notes on a piece of paper from his pocket.

"Um...Hi." Grace said trying to give her face some time to return to normal. James didn't look up from his note taking, but answered.

"Hey."

Grace shook her head. Didn't he know that she had been worried about him or that he was late? She looked for a clock to see what time it was, but couldn't find one in sight.

"Where have you been?" She asked with a hint of anger in her voice. James didn't respond at first and he still worked on whatever he was doing.

"I've been busy trying to get my portfolio together and finalized for tomorrow." Again he answered without looking up at her. That was evident to Grace as she rolled her eyes at him.

"James, you could have called me and told me you were going to be late for the bible study."

Now he looked up at Grace and saw that she stood with her arms crossed and her face and eyes reddened.

"Have you been crying?"

"No!"

"Well, you look like you have. Is everything ok?"

"Fine, it's just that…" She stopped and thought that James should know what is going on and she shouldn't have to tell him. Didn't he care that they had made plans for tonight?

"I have been packing all week and…"

Grace was cut off in mid sentence as James' cell phone rang and he answered it. Her shoulders dropped and she felt ignored. James resealed his portfolio and stood pacing the house as he talked. Grace sighed with a frustrated breath and watched him for a second. Then she saw his coat on the couch and went over to it; picking it up, she took it to the hall closet and hung it up. But before she closed the closet door, a small dark object fell from the inside pocket of the coat. Bending down, she took it in her hands. Her eyes searched for James, who was now in the kitchen still talking, she made sure he hadn't seen her. The small object was a box, a box that a ring would fit into.

No way it couldn't be, could it?? Grace's thoughts sped through notions of whatever could be in the small box. She had to open it and find out. Again she checked to see where James was in the house and satisfied with her investigation opened the black box. All her beliefs were true, a sparkling diamond solitaire gold ring sat snug within the box. Grace's heart began to flutter with joy and excitement. She couldn't believe it. He had bought a ring. Was he going to propose to her? When was he going to do it? Her mind raced with ideas and anticipation. The ring was amazing, the perfectly cut diamond dazzled back at her. Grace couldn't take her eyes off it. From the kitchen, James called out to Grace. Her eyes went wide and she froze in place.

Oh no, no! Snapping the box shut, Grace's hands fumbled and dropped it. James said her name again then started moving in her direction. Dropping to her knees she swept the floor of the closet reaching out for the box. James was coming closer.

No please! There, she put her hands on the small box, standing as fast as she could and closed the closet door. Going back into the living room, she sat on the couch and slid the small box into the couch cushions behind her, just as James entered the room.

"There you are. What were you doing?" Grace shook her head in innocence. She tried to sit casual and become relaxed.

Did he know what she had found? Quickly she asked to see his portfolio. A smile drew across James' face as he sat on the couch next to her and unzipped the brief case again. He opened to the first page and started explaining the projects to her. As he went through the portfolio page by page, Grace couldn't help but think about the ring. She still didn't believe that James had bought a ring. How did he afford something like this? He didn't have a job. Maybe he was banking on this interview a little too much. When James finished describing the last piece in his portfolio, he returned it to the floor next to him.

"So, what do you think? Do you think I've got a chance?" Grace nodded her head. Her mood had calmed down after she had found the ring. But, she was still a bit upset with James for not calling her.

"I was worried for you, when you didn't show tonight on time." James cast his eyes to the floor.

"Sorry, I just got caught up getting ready for tomorrow. This job will be an ultimate life change for me. This company is worldwide. I can progress higher than I ever dreamed." Grace gave a slight smile.

"Eventually, I'll be making some huge money and you can quit working for St. Luke's and start doing what you've always wanted." Grace felt under-appreciated by his words.

"James, I love what I do and wouldn't want anything else. It's the role God has set for me." She said in her own defense.

"You can't be serious? Haven't you ever wanted more? A bigger house, a nicer car?"

"You don't get me, do you?" She shot back. "I don't need those things to make me happy. God has given everything to me."

"No, He hasn't. He's taken everything away don't you see?"

That remark hit Grace in the heart. She looked away from him in hurtfulness. James knew he shouldn't have said what he did.

"No Grace, look I am sorry, I didn't mean..." He took her hands in his. "Listen I'm sorry, please." She looked at him with her eyes red again.

"What's happened to you?" She asked.

"Happened, what do you mean? I'm the same."

"No, you're not. All of a sudden ever since this job interview came up, you have been acting differently."

James took into account Grace's words. Had he been acting differently? He didn't think so.

"I'm sorry, ok? I've just been under a lot of stress lately with this interview coming up."

There he went again about the job interview. Grace thought, she was sick of hearing about it.

"Are you still going to come over tomorrow and help me pack after the interview? Or are you going to leave me waiting again?"

James must have known what she was thinking. He stood up and faced her. Tears ran down her face.

"Come on, let's go for a walk."

Was he crazy it was freezing outside? Why would he want to go for a walk now? She was so confused. Grace's mind came to a halt. *The ring!* It was still stashed behind her in the couch, how could she have forgotten.

"Where is my coat?" Grace's nerves where in panic. He was going to propose to her without a ring!

"I...um...hung it in the hall closet." James turned from her to get it. What was she going to do? Maybe she could slip it back into his pocket? Which pocket did he have it in? No, that wouldn't work.

The portfolio. Place the ring in the portfolio. On the floor the thick black leather briefcase laid at her feet. Would James notice? He would just think he misplaced it, right? Grace's mind swam in anxiety. No, they had just looked through the case and he would know it wasn't in there. Grace didn't know what to do.

The portfolio, just unzip it and slip it in there and then put it in his jacket later. Would that work, was he going to propose to her tonight? Grace reached down to the black case and unzipped a small opening. Taking the ring box in her hands carefully placing it over the opening, ready to drop it in the middle of the portfolio. James appeared in the room.

"Hey, I couldn't find your coat?" In a flash Grace repositioned herself on the couch, the ring box hidden in her hands, heart racing.

"Um...it's in my bedroom."

"Oh." James left the room in search of her coat.

Grace's eyes followed him till he was out of sight. Then she centered the ring box over the hole and dropped it in. She checked the case to make sure the bulge from the object would not be noticeable. Nothing. Perfectly normal. She let out a breath of relief. Standing as James returned with her own winter coat, he helped her pull it on.

Outside, the weather was just as cold as Grace had thought.

"James, it's really cold out here, please can we go in?" They had walked a good distance from behind the house toward the lake. Stopping at the edge of the frozen basin of water. James overlooked the icy lake into the woods beyond. He longed for the wilderness. It was cold, but he just wanted to run free amongst the pines and earth.

"Yeah, it is cold." The cool air was crisp and fresh, as the steam of his breath floated in front of him.

"Grace. Everything is going to be fine." He faced her now. She was beautiful as ever to him. Loose pieces of her blonde hair that hung from under a gray stocking hat blew in the frosty wind. It was hard for her to focus on the moment. Apprehension filled her being.

What if he proposed to her now? He wouldn't find the ring in his coat pocket. She shivered with a mixture of chills and nervousness trying to relax.

"Why are we out here?" She asked.
James took a deep breath. "I...just wanted to tell you that..."

Here it comes. Grace thought. She held her breath.

"I love you." James said locking his gaze with hers.
Grace let her breath out. The words made her heart pound with intensity. She let a smile slip over her face. Wrapping her arms around James neck she moved in closer to him.

"I love you too."

"I promise everything will be perfect with us." James put his hands around her waist.

"Yeah?" She said a bigger smile on her face.

"Whatever may come, wherever our lives lead, you and I will face it together."

He looked deep into her eyes and kissed her. Grace didn't hesitate and kissed him back. They warmed each other's souls in that bitter cold moment. Uniting the missing piece in both of their lives.

30

He had been up for hours, all dressed and ready to leave at any moment. Reserving enough time to review his portfolio before he left as well. But, the interview with Baxter and his people wasn't for quite a while. He didn't want anything getting in his way today. It was going to be a turning point in his life and he didn't want to blow it. Last night with Grace was an eye opener for him. Lately, all he could think was the interview and how he had been preparing for it. This was a chance of a lifetime and he hoped Grace understood that.

Now, with a cup of coffee in front of him and seat at the kitchen table, he cracked open his black leather bible and removed the bookmark where he had last left off. James should have done this a long time ago. Why hadn't he let God in on his remarkable opportunity? Probably because he was afraid of the answer. What if God was telling him that this position wasn't his true calling in life? James wasn't sure he could handle that. This was everything that he ever wanted. How could he be wrong? A career like this would give James a very prosperous life for him and Grace. They could raise a family together in a brand new house. They could eat at the finest restaurants and be invited to the best parties. The thoughts made James eager to meet his new boss and be introduced into his future colleagues. His mind ran through possibilities of topics that would impress the employer about him. He took a sip from his coffee. Even though the job opportunity had come through his uncle. James had to show them that he could earn the profession on his own merits. All of a sudden, a thought a popped into his head and he leapt from his spot at the kitchen table and moved to his computer trying not to lose the idea. On the way over, he must have bumped his leg on the edge of the table because his coffee mug came splashing down all over the neatly pressed shirt and pants. James cursed wildly at the accident. He checked the time and estimated he had an hour before the interview. He walked quickly back to his bedroom to change his outfit.

Grace had gotten through three boxes of items from her parent's room. It was an arduous process, but she wanted to be strong through it. She wished James were with her to support her as she went through her parents' things. Last night had really given her strength. She had a notion of why James didn't propose to her, it seemed that he was more overwhelmed with thoughts of the interview then she had realized. She would give him time to approach her in his own way. Although the warming kiss they had shared could have been all she needed, his simple confirmation of love to her, spoke to her soul and put her heart to rest. Nothing could break their love now. James' interview and possible career ahead of him was a good thing and she was glad for him. Grace just wanted James to make the right decision through God. She said a prayer to guide him in the correct way.

She opened a dresser drawer and removed it, dumping the contents on the bed beside her. Small trinkets of her parents, past and scraps of memories spilled out before her. A tiny smile shaped her mouth at the possessions. Organizing them into piles and placing them into another box carefully, Grace came across a small wooden box. Opening it, she found a small velvet bag inside. Excited with her secret find, she untied the bag and poured out its treasure into her hand. A petite silver ring shined dully back at her. It was her mother' promise ring. It had been given to her before her father could afford an engagement ring for his future bride. Grace closed her eyes and held it close. She had expected to find something like this amongst her parent's things. But, the sight of it now was tremendously emotional. It reminded her of how she had found James' engagement ring last night. She never said anything to him about it. But now, as she held the tiny silver ring in her hands, she had feelings of remorse about discovering the engagement ring. She had to call him, tell him that she had found the ring. Going to the kitchen and grabbing the phone, she dialed James' number. Holding the phone against her ear with her shoulder turned on the kitchen sink faucet. Running the beloved silver ring under the water to clean it, Grace jerked back at the surprisingly hot temperature of the water and dropped the ring. Circling the sink it slipped through the slits and down into the drain.

"No."

It was gone. The phone slipped from her shoulder and smashed to the ground breaking sending it into pieces.

With a new pair of pants on, James was hard at work trying to iron a new shirt. He heard the jingle of his cell phone from across the room. Already frustrated with his change of clothes the phone just annoyed him further.

Who could that be? Didn't they know he had an important day ahead of him? The phone rang out again. James let out an irritated groan. He slammed down the hot iron next to his shirt and went to retrieve his phone. Midway across the room the phone stopped ringing, by the time he got to it the call registered as missed on the phone's display. He cursed quietly. Flipping open the device and discovering that he had not one but two missed calls, but only one voice message was left. He called his voice mail and listened to the message.

"James, hello, its Ted Fuller from Mr. Baxter's office. We have arrived at the meeting location and we are sorry to tell you on such short notice, but we are going to need you here as soon as possible. Mr. Baxter's flight was moved to another airport and we are going to have to leave earlier than expected. So please make it here as quickly as you can. Thank you."

James checked the time of the message. It had been left ten minutes ago. How had he missed their call? He had better get moving, he had a small drive downtown ahead of him. He hastily checked the second missed call that had been posted. It was Grace's number. He didn't have time to talk to her. The shirt he had been ironing was as good as it was going to get. He unplugged the iron and threw on the shirt. Quickly, he knotted his tie as fast as he could, collected his car keys, wallet, phone and jacket.

Running for the door threw on the jacket and shut the door behind him. He stopped dead in his tracks and reopened the door. He stepped back inside and grabbed his black portfolio case. Cursing at the thought of forgetting it and not getting a chance to look it over one more time, he took the stairs down and the door outside to the parking lot. A wave of hard wind and snow hit him in his face just as he stepped out. A white blanket of snow covered everything.

Grace was distressed at the thought of losing her mother's promise ring. But, that wasn't all that was troubling her. As she dove deeper into her parent's room, she found more items of lost memories. The emotional strain was rapidly becoming more than she could handle.

She needed to calm down, take a break from packing. She went back to the kitchen and started a kettle of water for some warm tea.

The snow was blinding as James struggled to keep a good pace. This wasn't his fault; he had no control over the weather.

God was punishing him for some reason, he thought.

Doesn't He know this interview is everything? The mustang slid and skidded all over the road. He pumped the brakes a few time to regain control. The last thing James needed was to get stuck in a ditch. The interview's destination was only a few blocks more. He cursed again at his vehicle as it started to glide beyond his power. He was so close.

Grace heard the teakettle's whistle from the other room and she entered the kitchen to attend to her drink. She removed a mug from the cupboard and placed the tea bag inside it. Her mother loved hot tea in the winter. After pouring the hot water from the kettle, she dunked the bag and let her mind wander. She noticed the snow outside had stopped as she gazed out through her back window. She looked down at her simmering tea.

Wait. What was that?

Grace snapped her vision back to the window. It was hard to make out. She stared for a moment, not moving, but didn't see anything. Just white.

It was nothing. She thought. Slightly turning from the window she dunked her tea bag a few more times. Then one last time she swiftly peeked up.

There. She saw it more vividly, but brief and she knew what it was, someone in the woods behind her house. But, not just anyone, it was her mother!

James was glad to feel the warmth of the hotel lobby as he entered. With his portfolio in hand he walked to the front desk and waited for an employee.

Where were these stupid people? He had an appointment to make.

"James Mason." A voice called out. James twirled around as a man, his hand stretched out to him, came walking up toward him.

"Yeah." He gripped the man's hand firmly and confidently.

"Hi, Ted Fuller, everybody's in the next room waiting."

"How did you know it was me?" He asked the sharply dressed man.

"Well, you are the only guy that's walked in this place in the last few hours. I figured it was you also because you were carrying a portfolio." The man pointed at James' black case.

"Come on, we haven't got a lot of time."

James followed him into a small room off the lobby.

Grace pulled on her winter coat and hat as fast as she could. A string from her coat wrapped around her cross necklace tugging on it. She forced the coat on, not noticing her necklace break and fall from around her neck to the foyer floor.

Racing out through the front door, she was almost knocked down by the bitter cold wind. Moving around then to the back of the house was difficult because the ground was covered in snow and ice. She couldn't believe it, her mother. Could it really be her? She had to know.

James had now shook four different sets of hands, the last being Mr. James Baxter's. He knew it was a good sign having the same name as the corporate tycoon. It was amazing just to shake the man's hand. The four other men sat across a conference table with James on the opposite side. Everyone, but James, wore thousand dollar suits.

These guys smelled of money and luxury straight down to the cufflinks.

"James..." The CEO said. "I'll get right down to it. We are in need of a Boston based editing director and we think you are the man for the job." James was taken aback by the title and position. "Are you interested?" Thoughts of endless possibilities came to James' mind.

"Oh, yes indefinitely. But, I assumed you were in need of a person in this area."

"Nope, Boston is where you'll be stationed and let me tell you it's quite a town." Baxter slapped James on the back leaving his hand there a moment laughing to the group. James wondered if they got paid to laugh at the man's jokes?

But, James had never been to Boston before. What would Grace think about the location? Would she move with him? He had no idea the position was in Boston.

"Ok it's settled then. We just found ourselves a new editing director." The man laughed again, but James sensed something wasn't right. They hadn't even looked at his portfolio yet.

"Don't you want to look at my work before you hire me?" The four men looked amongst each other. Then Baxter's voice came again.

"Sure, sure we'll take a look."
James laid the black case on the table between them and slowly unzipped it.

There was no sight of anyone out in the woods that she could see. Grace couldn't take anymore of the cold and turned to retreat back inside.

Then she heard it. It was unmistakable, the tranquil sound of her mother's voice.

"Mom!" She called out. Again the voice came clearer. Did she hear right? Grace removed her hat and listened through the howling wind. Yes, yes she heard it, her name. But, she didn't see anyone. She couldn't believe it, her mother calling for her. Tears streamed down her cheeks. Then instantly there seemed to be nothing, no voices, and no names. How long had she been walking? What was she doing? It couldn't have been her. Was she seeing things?

"Mom?" She called out once more, nothing but emptiness.

All of a sudden, Grace slipped falling to her hands and knees. The ground beneath her trembled and then came an explicit cracking noise. Grace's heart beat wildly, her breathing stiffened. She knew now where she was. Struggling to stand, her feet slipped again and she came crashing down a second time. Another cracking noise came from beneath her. Terror buried her consciousness. She shut her eyes tight. Relentlessly fighting to move, more splitting sounds came from under her. The wet feeling of water soaked the knees of her pants. Grace shot open her eyes looking straight down. She could see right through the ice to the lake below her, ice fracturing in every direction she touched. Her lips quivered in fear.

Please Lord, rescue me. Grace felt a warming presence engulf her soul and bound her with love.

Oh Jesus.

Then the ice cracked one last time and Grace's body plunged into the freezing cold water.

So far Baxter and his three associates were impressed with James' portfolio. But, it wasn't until they reached the middle of the presentation they were really surprised by what they had found. They had all discovered a small black box. Immediately James knew what it was. Yet, how it had gotten in there was beyond any of his thoughts.

"Mason, what, were you trying to buy us off?" Baxter joked opening the small object. James didn't react to the men's remarks. All that was on his mind was Grace. It suddenly hit him like a bolt of lightning. He had it all wrong, going about the interview. She had asked him so many times why hadn't he listened to her? This position as an editing director wasn't what he wanted. He never wanted to move to Boston away from everyone. James hadn't taken into account his new life God had shown him in the woods during the retreat weekend. The men went on about the engagement ring laughing with each other. James had reverted to his old mentality. Striving for his own goals in life instead of what God was leading him to do. He didn't want job in Boston. He wanted to propose to Grace and love her for the rest of their lives. A career could come later.

James watched as the men on the other side of the table pointed out how tiny the diamond was. He reached across the table and snatched the engagement ring from Baxter's hands.

"No."

The man was caught off guard. James felt like he had just been given a decision. Either become one of these men or live a life by God's will.

"What?"

"No, I don't want this job."

James shut the box tight and slipped it into his jacket pocket. Puzzled looks came over the men's faces.

"I don't want this life."

They looked at one another bewildered at James' words.

"I choose Grace." With that James flew from the room.

James had never felt so alive more than he did right now. An abounding joy swept over him. Like a rocket he drove his mustang in search of Grace, his love, his life.

The red mustang skidded into the snow of Grace's driveway and came to a stop. Leaping from his vehicle, he made his way to the front door. He knocked twice.

Forget it just go in and take her in your arms. James twisted the knob and stepped into the foyer.

"Grace!" He called out looking for her. Something crunched beneath he shoes. Lifting his foot he bent down and picked up Grace's silver cross necklace.

Something's wrong! He shouted her name again. His mind racing over possibilities, the house was silent. Moving boxes everywhere.

Why didn't you just help her pack today? James was still irritated with himself at his attitude the last few weeks. He clutched the cross necklace in his hand. Checked Grace's bedroom; he found nothing. He moved through the kitchen to her parent's bedroom. All he found was clothes and items strewn about the room.

Wait!

James went back to the kitchen and peered out through the back window.

"Dear God, NO!"

James burst from the house and circled it. His feet fumbling as he moved through the snow. Tripping over himself in haste, he quickly regained his footing and traveled as fast he could to the hole in the lake. The ice under him creaked and cracked as he carefully stepped on the lake's edge. His steamy breath showed the rate of his anticipation. He froze solid as slivers of ice split beneath his feet. He could see her, she was right in front of him, halfway in the water. Her body was motionless, pale. His instincts told him he probably have a minute or less to recover her before the whole lake collapsed in. James took a deep breath and lingered a second planning his rescue.

Go! Moving with swiftness he reached Grace and with remarkable strength freed her from the icy water. Suddenly, his foot broke through the ice tripping him up. But it didn't stop his determination; he loosened it and made a dash to safety. Out of breath he cradled Grace's soaked body in his arms tears moving down his face. James closed his eyes and prayed.

31

The spring brought glowing colors and budding new life. Everything seemed to be bright and alive. A contribution from God or so, James thought. On this particular day, the color of choice was white. St. Luke's seemed to be covered in it. And as for today, it was fitting since it was the wedding of Thomas and Jan. Although the ceremony was over the celebration was just beginning.

It was moments like these that James missed Grace the most. He wished he could hold her in his arms, tell her he loved her, but she was gone, home with Jesus. On that day the emergency personnel said it was hypothermia.

The reception was outdoors under large tents each decorated to perfection. They had been set up behind the church on a newly designed stone lot just for occasions such as this. But, that wasn't the only new structure St. Luke's had. Because of the recently formed "Grace Fund", that Nelson and Thomas collaborated and donated on, St. Luke's was getting the face-lift it was sorely in need of. The most amazing part was how the "Grace Fund" brought out the many lives she had touched during her time. James only hoped he could connect with half as many in his new position as head of the LIFT youth group, let alone the amount she had. People from all over the city and even a few from out of state had given to the church. And each Sunday collections were made and then tallied by a selected group at Thomas' company. All it took was some financial backing, Nelson arranged through his bank. Father Warren couldn't have been happier to see his flock grow by such leaps and bounds. It was just so heartbreaking it had to come through a loss of one of the most beautiful worshipers.

Now, as everyone took his or her seats at the appointed tables, James stood and looked at everyone. Grace would have loved to see everyone here and they all missed her the same. He brought the microphone to his mouth and spoke.

"First, I want to say what a incredible ceremony that was." James looked over at his uncle who sat next to him and then at Jan. "Jan you look spectacular today...and Thomas you don't look so bad yourself." The crowd laughed contently at the joke. Thomas gave his nephew a proud smile.

"Not everyone could be with us today..." A short silence passed.

"Yet, the presence of God was in full effect and sometimes God gives you a twist that you never quite expect. But, you're in no way meant to. That is how He works through our lives."

James eyed his uncle and the new bride again.

"Intertwining His love with remarkable connections, no matter how big or small, good or bad that they may be; that's why it's called grace. He's the only one who could have created it and given it to us." James lifted his glass.

"To Thomas and Jan, may God's grace bless their lives and may they follow Him where ever He may lead."